***Look at me*, Raoul silently commanded again.**

Sirena's lips drained of color and her hand trembled as she reached out, trying to find the gate. She stared straight ahead, eyes blinking and blinking—

"She's fainting!" He shoved past his lawyers and toppled chairs to reach her even as her own lawyer turned and reacted.

Raoul shouted for First Aid.

Someone appeared with oxygen in a blessedly short time. He let himself be pushed back a half-step, but he couldn't take his eyes off the way Sirena's cheeks had gone hollow, her skin gray. Everything in him—breath, blood, thought—ground to a halt as he waited for a sign that she would be okay.

Distantly he heard the attendant asking about pre-existing conditions and Raoul racked his brain. She wasn't diabetic, had never taken any medication that he'd seen. He'd reached for the phone he'd turned off while court was in session, intent on accessing her personnel file, when he heard her lawyer answer in a low murmur.

"She's pregnant."

The words burst like shattered glass in his ears.

Dani Collins discovered romance novels in high school and immediately wondered how a person trained and qualified for *that* amazing job. She married her high school sweetheart, which was a start, then spent two decades trying to find her fit in the wide world of romance writing, always coming back to Harlequin Mills & Boon®.

Two children later, and with the first entering high school, she placed in Harlequin's *Instant Seduction* contest. It was the beginning of a fabulous journey towards finally getting that dream job.

When she's not in her Fortress of Literature, as her family calls her writing office, she works, chauffeurs children to extra-curricular activities, and gardens with more optimism than skill. Dani can be reached through her website at www.danicollins.com

Recent titles by the same author:

MORE THAN A CONVENIENT MARRIAGE?
PROOF OF THEIR SIN
  (One Night With Consequences)
NO LONGER FORBIDDEN?

Did you know these are also available as eBooks?
Visit www.millsandboon.co.uk

A DEBT PAID IN PASSION

BY

DANI COLLINS

Published in Great Britain 2014
by Mills & Boon, an imprint of Harlequin (UK) Limited,
Eton House, 18-24 Paradise Road, Richmond, Surrey, TW9 1SR

© 2014 Dani Collins

ISBN: 978 0 263 24167 9

Harlequin (UK) Limited's policy is to use papers that are natural,
renewable and recyclable products and made from wood grown in
sustainable forests. The logging and manufacturing processes conform
to the legal environmental regulations of the country of origin.

Printed and bound in Great Britain
by CPI Antony Rowe, Chippenham, Wiltshire

B000 000 011 1390

A DEBT PAID
IN PASSION

Generous readers, you're my Valentines.

Thank you for making
all those hours in my stuffy attic writing room worth it.

CHAPTER ONE

LOOK AT ME, Raoul Zesiger willed Sirena Abbott.

He had to lean back in his chair to see her past the three men between them. He should have been looking at the judge, but he couldn't take his eyes off Sirena.

She sat very still, face forward, her profile somber. Her absurdly long gypsy lashes had stayed downswept as his lawyer had risen to speak. She didn't even flick a glance in his direction when her own lawyer stood to plead that jail time was counterproductive, since she needed to work to pay back the stolen funds.

Raoul's lawyers had warned him this wouldn't result in incarceration, but Raoul had pressed hard for it. He would see this treacherously innocent-looking woman, with her mouth pouted in grave tension and her thick brunette locks pulled into a deceptively respectful knot, go to jail for betraying him. For stealing.

His stepfather had been a thief. He had never expected to be taken advantage of again, especially by his reliable PA, a woman he'd come to trust to be there, always. But she had dipped her fingers into his personal account.

Then she had tried to manipulate him into going easy by *being* easy.

He didn't want the flash of memory to strike. His ears were waiting for the judge to state that this would progress to a sentence, but his body prickled with heat as he recalled the feel of those plump lips softening under his. Her breasts, a lush handful, had smelled of summer. Her nipples were sun-warmed berries against his tongue, succulent and sweet. The heart-shaped backside he'd watched too often as it retreated from his office had been both taut and smooth as he had lifted her skirt and peeled lace down. Thighs like powdered sugar, an enticing musky perfume between that pulled him to hard attention as he remembered how tight—almost virginal—she'd been. But so hot and welcoming.

Because she'd known her criminal act was about to come to light.

His gut clenched in a mixture of fury and unparalleled carnal hunger. For two years he'd managed to keep his desire contained, but now that he'd had her, all he could think about was having her again. He hated her for having such power over him. He could swear under oath that he'd never hurt a woman, but he wanted to crush Sirena Abbott. Eradicate her. Destroy her.

The clap of a gavel snapped him back to the courtroom. It was empty save for the five of them behind two tables, both facing the judge. His lawyer gave Raoul a resigned tilt of his head and Raoul realized with sick disgust that the decision had gone in Sirena's favor.

At the other table, partly obscured by her lawyer, Sirena's spine softened in relief. Her wide eyes lifted to the heavens, shining with gratitude. Her lawyer thanked the judge and set a hand under Sirena's elbow to help her rise, leaning in to say something to her.

Raoul felt a clench of possessiveness as he watched the solicitous middle-aged lawyer hover over her. He told himself it was anger, nothing else. He loathed being a victim again. She shouldn't get away with a repayment plan of six hundred pounds a month. That wasn't reparation. That was a joke.

Why wouldn't she look at him? It was the least she could do: look him in the eye and acknowledge they both knew she was getting away with a crime. But she murmured something to her lawyer and left the man packing his briefcase as she circled to the aisle. Her sexy curves were downplayed by her sleek jacket and pencil skirt, but she was still alluring as hell. Her step slowed as she came to the gate into the gallery.

Look at me, Raoul silently commanded again, holding his breath as she hesitated, sensing she was about to swing her gaze to his.

Her lips drained of color and her hand trembled as she reached out, trying to find the gate. She stared straight ahead, eyes blinking and blinking—

"She's fainting!" He shoved past his two lawyers and toppled chairs to reach her even as her own lawyer turned and reacted. They caught her together.

Raoul hated the man anew for touching her as they both eased her to the floor. She was dead weight. He had to catch her head as it lolled. She hadn't been this insubstantial the last time he'd held her. She hadn't been *fragile.*

Raoul barked for first aid.

Someone appeared with oxygen in blessedly short time. He let himself be pushed back a half step, but he couldn't take his eyes off the way Sirena's cheeks had gone hollow, her skin gray. Everything in him, breath, blood, thought, ground to a halt as he waited for a new verdict: that she would be okay.

It was his father all over again. The lack of response, the wild panic rising in him as he fought against helplessness and brutal reality. Was she breathing? She couldn't be dead. *Open your eyes, Sirena.*

Distantly he heard the attendant asking after preexisting conditions and Raoul racked his brain. She wasn't diabetic, had never taken medication that he'd seen. He reached for the phone he'd turned off while court was in session, intent on accessing her personnel file, when he heard her lawyer answer in a low murmur.

"She's pregnant."

The words burst like shattered glass in his ears.

Sirena became aware of something pressed to her face. Clammy sweat coated her skin and a swirl of her ever-present nausea turned mercilessly inside her.

She lifted a heavy hand to dislodge whatever was smothering her and a voice said, "You fainted, Sirena. Take it easy for a minute."

Opening her eyes, she saw John, the highly recom-mended lawyer who'd been perfunctory until she'd almost vomited in his wastebasket. She'd told him the father's identity was irrelevant, but Raoul was glaring from be-yond John's shoulder with all the relevance of an unfor-giving sun on a lost soul in the desert—and he appeared about as sympathetic.

She had tried hard not to look at Raoul, former boss, brief lover, unsuspecting father. He was too…everything. Tall, dark, unabashedly urbane and sophisticated. Severe. Judgmental.

But of their own accord, her hungry eyes took in his appearance—her first opportunity to do so in weeks. She cataloged his razor-sharp charcoal suit, the solid black tie. His jaw was freshly shaved for his morning appointment, his dark hair recently cut into the sternly simple style of a successful businessman.

And there were his eyes, the gray irises stormy and full of condemnation as they snared hers in an unbreak-able stare.

John asked, "Is there any pain? We've called an am-bulance."

Sirena flashed a terrified glance back at Raoul. It was

a mistake. She realized immediately that he'd read it for what it was: an admission of guilt. A betrayal of truth.

Clenching her perfidious eyes closed, she willed him not to pick up on what had been revealed, but he was the most acutely intelligent person she'd ever met. He missed nothing.

If he knew she was carrying his baby, there'd be another fight. Considering what this current contest had taken out of her, she wasn't ready for another. She wouldn't, *couldn't,* let him think he had a right to custody of her child.

"Sirena," Raoul said in that dark chocolate voice of his.

Her skin rippled in a pleasurable shiver of recognition. Two years of hearing every intonation in that voice left her with the knowledge that her name on his lips right now was an implacable warning.

"Look at me," he commanded.

Sirena reached blindly for John's hand, clenching her icy fingers on his warm, dry ones. Beneath the oxygen mask, her voice was hollow and whisper thin.

"Tell him to leave me alone or I'll take out a restraining order."

CHAPTER TWO

THE FIRST VOLLEY of the second war was waiting when she got home from the hospital. More tests had been scheduled, but for the moment her doctor was putting her faint down to stress and low blood sugar resulting from her unrelenting nausea.

Sirena thought nothing could be more stressful than facing prison while dealing with an unplanned pregnancy, but Raoul knew no bounds when it came to psychological torture. She read the email John had forwarded:

My client has every reason to believe your client carries his baby. He insists on full involvement in the care through pregnancy and will take sole custody at birth.

Her blood congealed, even though this was no surprise. Raoul was possessive. She'd learned *that*. This reaction was fully expected, but having anyone try to take this baby from her was unthinkable.

Blinking the sting of desperation from her eyes, she typed, It's not his, saying aloud, "And tell him to go to hell."

She didn't let herself dwell on the fact that Raoul wanted his baby. It would make her weaken toward a man she needed to believe was a monster—even though she'd spent two years falling into deep infatuation with not just a dynamic tycoon, but a man who was a caring son and protective older stepbrother. In some ways he was her mirror image, she'd often thought fancifully. They'd both lost a parent and both wanted the best for their younger siblings. She had come to believe him to be an admirable person with a dry wit and standards that put her learned habits of perfectionism to shame.

No, she reminded herself as she prepared a slice of toast she would force herself to eat. He was a cruel, angry, small person who felt nothing. For her, at least. He'd proven it when he'd made passionate love to her one day, then had her arrested the next.

A black hole of despair threatened to open beneath her feet, but she was safe now. That part was over. She'd made a horrible mistake and the judge had accepted her remorse, even if Raoul hadn't. She had no idea how she would come up with six hundred pounds a month, but that was a minor worry against convincing Raoul the baby wasn't his.

There was no way she could live with having another loved one wrenched from her life. The fear of her baby growing up without its mother, the way she had, had given her the strength to fight tooth and nail against Raoul's determination to put her in jail. Somehow she would rally the strength to oust him from her life for good.

Which left her feeling incredibly bereft, but she ignored it.

Taking tea, toast and a tablet for nausea to the sofa, she scanned her laptop to see if any transcription jobs had come in. The legal bills were appalling and being fired three months ago had decimated her very modest savings.

If only she could take back that one awful moment when she had thought, *Raoul will understand.* She rubbed her brow where it crinkled in lament. Borrowing from him had seemed the most simple and obvious thing to do when her sister had been in tears, saying, *I guess I'm not meant to be a teacher.* Their father was expecting payment from a big customer any day. Ali had struggled so hard to get her marks up and be accepted into the specialized program. The tuition was due, but the cash was not in hand.

I can cover it, Sirena had assured her, confident the balance would move out and come back into Raoul's account on the same statement. He probably wouldn't even notice, let alone care. He paid *her* to worry about little details like that.

Then her father's customer had gone insolvent.

Not overnight, of course. It started with a delay of a few more days. A week. Sirena had begun chasing it herself, right up to the monthly cutoff date, not wanting to mention her self-approved loan to her boss until she had the funds to repay it.

The money hadn't appeared and the opportunity to explain hadn't arisen, not before other events.

And since she didn't want to involve her father when his livelihood was nose-diving, she had shouldered the fallout herself, keeping her motives from Raoul and not revealing to her family what she'd done or that she was facing jail time for it.

This had been the most crushingly lonely and frightening time of her life.

A muted beep announced an incoming email. From Raoul. Her heart leaped in misplaced anticipation. It was one word.

Liar.

He wasn't buying that the baby wasn't his.

Gritting her teeth against an ache that crushed her chest, she added Raoul to her email block list and sent a missive to John.

Tell him that contacting me directly is out of line. If the baby was his, I would sue for support. I would have asked for leniency when he was trying to put me in jail. This baby is not his and he must LEAVE ME ALONE.

Hitting send was like poking herself in the throat. She drew a pained breath, fighting the sense of loss. But life hit you with sudden changes and you had to roll with them. She had learned that when her mother had died, and again when her stepmother had whisked her father and half sister to Australia with brutal speed as soon as Sirena graduated and enrolled in business school.

People *left*, was what she'd learned. They disappeared from your life whether you wanted them to or not. Sometimes they even fired you and tried to lock you away in prison so they'd never have to see you again.

Making a disgusted noise at herself for indulging in what amounted to emotional self-harm, she turned her thoughts to the little being who wouldn't leave her. With a gentle hand on her unsettled abdomen, she focused on the one person she'd do everything in her power to keep in her life forever. She didn't intend to smother the poor thing, just be his or her mother. She couldn't countenance anyone taking that role from her. And Raoul would try. He was that angry and ruthless.

She shivered as she recalled seeing that side of him for the first time, after making bail. The only thing that had gotten her through the humiliating process of being arrested, fingerprinted and charged was the certainty that Raoul didn't know what was happening to her. Some accountant had done this. A bank official. They didn't understand that Raoul might be gruff on the outside, but she was his best PA ever. His right hand. They'd become intimate. He would be furious that she was being treated this way.

She had believed with all her heart that as soon as she told him what had happened, he'd make it right.

He hadn't. He'd made her wait in the rain at the gate of his mansion outside London, eventually striding out with hard-hearted purpose, his severe expression chilly with distaste as he surveyed her.

"I've been trying to reach you," Sirena had said through the rungs of the security gate, frightened by how unreachable he seemed. "I was arrested today."

"I know," Raoul replied without a shred of concern. "I filed the complaint."

Her shock and stunned anguish must have been obvious, but his mouth had barely twitched in reaction. Cruel dislike had been the only emotion in his scathing expression. Sirena's stepmother had been small and critical, but she hadn't outright hated Sirena. In that second, she realized Raoul reviled her, and that was more painful than anything.

Guilt and remorse had made her want to shrivel up and die, but she couldn't—wouldn't—believe she'd ruined her career and her budding relationship with the man of her dreams over one tiny misstep.

"But…" Everything she wanted to say backed up in her throat. They'd developed friendship, reliance and respect over two years of working together and just yesterday they'd taken that relationship to a new level. He'd been tender and teasing and…

God, she had believed he'd been *loving.*

"But what?" he challenged. "You thought sleeping with me would make a difference to how I'd react when I found out you had stolen from me? I was bored. You were there. That's all yesterday was. You ought to know better than to think it would make me go easy on someone who was cheating me. Get a lawyer. You need one."

Swallowing the rock that her crust of toast had become,

Sirena pushed the betrayal firmly away. Raoul was in her past and somehow she had to make a future for herself and her baby. She turned her attention to putting out more feelers for work.

But over the next several weeks, the attacks from Raoul kept coming. Settlement offers that increased in size. Demands for paternity tests. Time limits.

Pacing John's office, she bit back a rebuke at him for revealing her pregnancy that day in the courtroom. She hadn't admitted to anyone that Raoul was the father and she was determined she never would.

"Here's what I would like to know, John. How am I supposed to pay more legal bills I can't afford when it's not even my wish to be talking to you about this?"

"Your wish may be coming true, Sirena. He's stated clearly that this is his final offer and you're to accept it by Monday or forever go empty-handed."

She stopped and stilled. Loss again. Like watching the final sands drifting through the neck of an hourglass, unable to stop them. Pain in her lip made her aware she was biting it to keep from crying out in protest. Rubbing her brow with a shaking hand, Sirena told herself it was what she wanted: Raoul gone from her life.

"Look, Sirena, I've told you several times this isn't my area of expertise. So far that hasn't mattered because you've refused to admit the baby is his—"

"It's not," she interjected, keeping her back to him. She wasn't a great liar and didn't like doing it, but she justified it because this baby was *hers.* Full stop.

"He obviously thinks it's possible. You and he must have been involved."

"Involvement comes in different levels, doesn't it?" she snapped, then closed her mouth, fearful she was saying too much.

"So you're punishing him for bringing less to the relationship than you did?"

"His mistresses spend more on an evening gown and he tried to send me to prison for it!" she swung around to blurt. "What kind of relationship is that?"

"You're punishing him for his legal action, then? Or not buying you a dress?"

"I'm not punishing him," Sirena muttered, turning back to the window overlooking a wet day in Hyde Park.

"No, you're punishing your child by keeping its father out of the picture—whether that father is Raoul Zesiger or some other nameless man you've failed to bring forward. I'm a father, so even though I don't practice family law, I know the best interests of the child are not served by denying a parent access just because you're angry with him. Do you have reason to believe he'd be an unfit parent?"

Completely the opposite, she silently admitted as a tendril of longing curled around her heart. She had seen how Raoul's stepsister adored him and how he indulged the young woman with doting affection while setting firm boundaries. Raoul would be a supportive, protective, exceptional father.

Her brows flinched and her throat tightened. She *was* angry with him. And secretly terrified that her child would ultimately pick its father over its mother, but that didn't justify keeping the baby from knowing both its parents.

"Have you thought about your child's future?" John prodded. "There are certain entitlements, like a good education, inheritances…"

She had to get this baby delivered first. That's where her focus had really been these last several weeks.

Sirena's fists tightened under her elbows as she hunched herself into a comfortless hug. Her mother had died trying to give birth to the baby who would have been Sirena's little brother. Sirena's blood pressure was under constant monitoring. Between that and the lawyer meetings, she was barely working, barely making the bills. The stress was making the test results all the more concerning.

She tried not to think of all the bad things that could happen, but for the first time she let herself consider what her child would need if she couldn't provide it. Her father and sister were all the way in Australia. It would be days before they could get here—if her stepmother let either of them come at all. Right now Faye was taking the high ground, sniffing with disapproval over Sirena's unplanned, unwed pregnancy. No one would be as emotionally invested as the baby's father...

"Sirena, I'm not trying to—"

"Be my conscience?" she interjected. He was still acting as one. "I have a specialist appointment on Monday. I don't know how long it will take. Tell him I will give his offer my full attention after that and will be in touch by the end of next week."

John's demeanor shifted. "So he is the father."

"That will be determined by the paternity test once the baby is born, won't it?" Sirena retorted, scrambling to hold onto as many cards as she could because she was running out of them, fast.

Raoul's mind had been going around in circles for weeks, driving him mad. If Sirena was pregnant with his child, she would have used that to keep him from trying to incarcerate her. Since she hadn't, it must not be his. But she could have used her condition for leniency during the proceedings and hadn't. Which meant she wanted to keep the pregnancy from him. Which led him to believe the baby was his.

Most troubling, if he wasn't the father, who was?

Raoul sent baleful glances around his various offices as he traveled his circuit of major cities, aware there were a plethora of men in his numerous office towers with whom Sirena, with her voluptuous body and warm smile, could easily have hooked up.

The thought grated with deep repugnance. He'd never heard the merest whisper of promiscuity about his PA, but she'd obviously led a secretive life. It wasn't as if she'd been a virgin when he'd made love to her.

She'd been the next thing to it, though, with her shy hesitancy that had turned to startled pleasure.

Biting back a groan, he tried not to think of that afternoon in a house he'd toured as a potential real estate investment. Every day he fought the recollection of their passionate encounter and every night she revisited him, her silky hair whispering against his skin, her soft giggle of self-consciousness turning to a gasp of awe as she stroked him. The hum of surrender in her throat as he found the center of her pleasure nearly had him losing it in his sleep.

Every morning he reminded himself he'd used a condom.

One that had been in his wallet so long he couldn't remember when or for whom he'd placed it there. He'd only been grateful to find it when a downpour had turned Sirena from the open front door into his arms. A stumbling bump of her pivoting into him, a gentlemanly attempt to keep her on her feet, a collision of soft curves against a body already charged with sexual hunger.

When she'd looked up at him with wonder as her abdomen took the impression of his erection, when she'd parted her lips and looked at his mouth as though she'd been waiting her whole life to feel it cover her own...

Swearing, Raoul rose to pace his Paris office. It was as far as he was willing to get from London after trying to settle with Sirena once and for all. The remembered vision of her passion-glazed eyes became overlaid with a more recent one: when her lawyer had mentioned her pregnancy and she had shot that petrified look at Raoul.

The baby was his. He knew it in his gut and if he'd been ruthless with her for stealing money, she had no idea the lengths he'd go for his child.

Doubt niggled, though. If the baby was his, and she was the type to embezzle, then try to sleep her way out of it, why wasn't she trying to squeeze a settlement out of him?

None of it added up and he was losing his mind trying to make sense of it. If she'd only *talk* to him. They used to communicate with incredible fluidity, finishing each other's sentences, filling in gaps with a look...

Lies, he reminded himself. All an act to trick him into trusting her, and it had worked. That's what grated so badly. He'd failed to see that she was unreliable, despite his history with shameless charlatans.

And how the hell had he turned into his father? Was it genetic that he should wind up sexually infatuated with his secretary? He'd successfully ignored such attractions for years. His father had killed himself over an interoffice affair, so he'd made it a personal rule to avoid such things at all costs. It was a matter of basic survival.

His surge of interest in Sirena had been intense right from the beginning, though. He'd hired her in spite of it, partly because he'd been sure he was a stronger man than his father. Maybe he'd even been trying to prove it.

It galled him that he'd fallen into a tryst despite his better intentions. But he might have come to terms with that failing if she hadn't betrayed him. Suddenly he'd been not just his father, but his mother, naively watching the bank account drain while being fed sweet, reassuring words to excuse it.

I was going to pay it back before you found out.

He tried to close out the echo of Sirena's clear voice, claiming exactly what any dupe would expect to hear once she realized her caught hands were covered in red. That he'd seen her as steadfast until that moment left him questioning his own judgment, which was a huge kick to his confidence. People relied on him all over the world. His weakness for her made him feel as though he was misrepresenting himself, and more than anything he hated being let down. It galled him. Mere repayment wasn't good enough to compensate for that. People like her needed to be taught a lesson.

Staring at his desktop full of work, he cursed the concentration he'd lost because of all this, the time wasted on legal meetings that could have been spent on work.

And the worst loss of production was because he was trying to replace the best PA he'd ever had!

Seemingly the best. His only comfort was that he hadn't given her the executive title he'd been considering. The damage she could have done in a position like that was beyond thinking. She was doing enough harm to his bottom line no longer employed by him at all.

It couldn't go on. He'd finally, reluctantly, sent her a strongly worded ultimatum and his palms were sweating that she would reject this one, too. She knew him well enough to believe that when he said final, he meant final, but he'd never had anything so valuable as his flesh and blood on the table. If she refused again…

She wouldn't. Sirena Abbott was more avaricious than he'd given her credit for, but she was innately practical. She would recognize he'd hit his limit and would cash in.

As if to prove it, his email blipped with a message from his lawyer.

Sirena Abbott had an appointment on Monday and wanted the rest of the week to think things through.

Raoul leaned on hands that curled into tight fists. His inner being swelled with triumph. Silly woman. When he said Monday, he meant *Monday*.

* * *

As Sirena entered the alcove that housed the front of her building, she was still preoccupied by the lecture from the obstetrician about taking time to relax. She needed to read up on side effects of the medication he'd prescribed, too.

Distracted, she didn't notice anyone until a lean, masculine body stepped out of the shadows. Her pulse leaped in excited recognition even as she jerked in alarm.

Her keys dropped with a clatter. Pressing herself into the glass door, she pulled her collar tighter to her throat. His familiar scent overwhelmed her, spicy and masculine beneath a layer of rain. The late-afternoon gloom threw forbidding shadows into the angles of his features and turned his short, spiky lashes into sharp blades above turbulent eyes. He was compelling as ever and she was as susceptible as always.

"Hello, Sirena."

That voice.

"What are you doing here?" Her knuckles dug into her neck where her pulse raced with dangerous speed. She was supposed to be avoiding this sort of elevation of her heart rate, but Raoul had always done this to her. Thank God she'd spent two years perfecting how to hide her girlish flushes of awareness and awestruck admiration. With a tilt of her chin she conveyed that he didn't intimidate her— even though she was in danger of cracking the glass at her back, she was pressed so hard against it.

"You didn't really think I'd wait until Friday," he said, uncompromising and flinty.

"I didn't think you'd be waiting at my door," she protested, adding with admirable civility, "I'll review the documents tomorrow, I promise."

Raoul shook his head in condescension. "Today, Sirena."

"It's been a long day, Raoul. Don't make it longer." Her

voice was weighted with more tiredness than she meant to reveal.

His eyes narrowed. "What sort of appointment did you have? Doctor?"

A little shiver of premonition went through her. Something told her not to let him see how unsettling the news had been, but the reality of all those tests and personal history forms had taken a toll. If she had thought she could avoid signing a shared custody agreement with Raoul, today she'd learned it was imperative she do so.

"Is the baby all right?" Raoul demanded gruffly. The edgy concern in his tone affected her, making her soften and stiffen at the same time.

"The baby is fine," she said firmly. If the mother could keep herself healthy enough to deliver—and ensure there was at least one parent left to rear it—the baby was in a great position for a long and happy life.

"You?" he questioned with sharp acuity. Damned man never missed a thing.

"I'm tired," she prevaricated. "And I have to use the loo. It's only five o'clock. That gives me seven hours. Come back at eleven fifty-nine."

Raoul's jaw hardened. "No." Leaning down, brushing entirely too close to her legs, he picked up her keys and straightened. "No more games, no more lawyers. You and I are hammering this out. Now."

Sirena tried to take her keys, but Raoul only closed his hand over them, leaving her fingers brushing the hard strength of his knuckles.

The contact sent an electric zing through her nervous system, leaving her entire body quivering over what was a ridiculously innocuous touch.

She'd been too stressed and nauseous to have sexual feelings these last months, but suddenly every vessel in her body came alive to the presence of *this* man, the aveng-

ing god who had never had any genuine respect for her in
the first place.

Tamping down on the rush of hurt and disappointment
that welled in her chest, Sirena found her spine, standing
up to him as well as a woman in flats could to a man who
was head and shoulders taller than she was.

"Let's get something clear," she said, voice trembling
a bit. She hoped he put it down to anger, not weak, stupid
longing for something that had never existed. "Whatever
agreement we come to is contingent on paternity tests
proving you're the father."

Raoul rocked back on his heels. His negotiation face slid
into place over his shock. In the shadowed alcove, Sirena
wasn't sure if his pupils really contracted to pinpoints, but
she felt his gaze like a lance that held her in place. It made
her nervous, but she was proud of herself for taking him
aback. She couldn't afford to be a pushover.

"Who else is in the running?" he gritted out.

"I have a life beyond your exalted presence." The lies
went up like umbrellas, but she had so few advantages.

He stood unflinching and austere, but there was something in his bearing that made her heart pang. She knew
he was the father, but by keeping him guessing she was
performing a type of torture on him, keeping him in a
state of anxious inability to act. It was cruel and made
her feel ashamed.

Don't be a wimp, Sirena. He could take care of himself.
The only thing she needed to worry about was her baby.

"Let's get this done," she said.

CHAPTER THREE

RAOUL HAD NEVER been in Sirena's flat. When he entered he was surprised to immediately feel as though he was returning to a place both familiar and comfortable. It was so *her*.

She was a tidy person with simple taste, but her innate sensuality came through in textures and easy blends of color. The open-plan lounge-kitchen was tiny, but everything had a place, houseplants were lush and well tended. Family snapshots smiled from walls and shelves. He had time while she was in the powder room to take in the miniscule bedroom kept as scrupulously neat as the rest, the bed notably a single.

Sirena cast him a harried glance as she emerged and shrugged from her coat, draping it over the back of a dining chair.

Her figure, voluptuous as ever, had a new curve that made him draw in a searing breath. Until this moment, *pregnant* had been a word bandied through hostile emails and legal paperwork. As he cataloged the snug fit of leggings and a stretchy top over a body that hadn't filled out much except in the one place, he felt his scalp tighten.

Sirena was carrying a baby.

Her pale, slender hand opened over the small bump. Too small? He had no idea about these things.

Yanking his gaze to her face, he saw defensive wariness

and something else, something incredibly vulnerable that triggered his deepest protective instincts.

Thankfully she glanced away, thick hair falling across her cheek to hide her expression. Raoul regrouped, reminding himself not to let her get to him, but he couldn't take his eyes off that firm swelling. He'd spent two years fighting the urge to touch this woman, had given in to a moment of weakness once, and it took all his self-discipline not to reach for her now. His hands itched to start at that mysterious bump then explore the rest of her luscious shape. He shoved his fists into his overcoat pockets and glared with resentment.

"I'm having ice water and an orange. Do you want coffee?" she asked.

"Nothing," he bit out. No more foot dragging. He was still reeling from her coy remark about paternity, played out so well he was entertaining a shred of uncertainty. He couldn't begin to consider what he'd do if he wasn't the father.

The not knowing made him restless, especially because he couldn't understand why she was tormenting him. Yes, his position would be strengthened if she admitted he was the father, but so would hers. He would do anything for his child. One glimpse of a pregnant belly shouldn't affect him this deeply, but all he could think was that his entire life had changed. Every decision from now on would be weighed against its effect on that tiny being in Sirena's center.

She took her frosted glass and plate of sectioned orange to the table, opening a file as she sat down. One glance invited him to take the chair across from her. They didn't stand on ceremony. He didn't hold her chair; this wasn't a date. It was reminiscent of the times they'd planted themselves on either side of a boardroom table and worked through projects and tasks until he'd cleared his plate and loaded hers full, confident it would all be completed to his exacting specifications.

He tightened his mouth against a blurted demand for answers. *Why?* If she had needed money, why hadn't she asked him for a loan? A raise? The salary he'd been paying her was generous, but he'd seen she was ready for more responsibility and the compensation that went with it. Had *this* been her plan all along? Pregnancy and a custody settlement?

The thought occurred as she opened the file and he glimpsed a copy of a contract filled with notations and scribbles.

"You *have* read it," he said with tight disgust.

"I do my homework, same as you," she retorted, ice clinking as she sipped. Her skin, fine grained as a baby's, was pale. Weren't pregnant women supposed to glow? Sirena didn't look unhealthy, but there were shadows under her eyes and in them. She touched her brow where she used to complain of tension headaches. He could see the pulse in her throat pounding as if her heart would explode.

The precariousness of his position struck him. He wanted to be ruthless, but not only was he facing a woman in a weakened condition, her condition affected a baby. As he absorbed the raised stakes, his tension increased. The scent of the fresh orange seemed overly strong and pungent.

"I want medical reports," he said with more harsh demand than he would typically use at the opening of a negotiation.

Sirena flinched and laced her fingers together. Without looking at him, she said, "I don't have a problem sharing the baby's health checkups. So far it's been textbook. I have a scan on my laptop I can email you once we've signed off." Now her eyes came up, but her gaze was veiled. She was hiding something.

"Who are you?" he muttered. "You're not the Sirena I knew." His PA had been approachable and cheerful, quick to smile, quick to see the humor in things. This woman was locked down, serious and more secretive than he'd ever imagined.

Like him, which was a disturbing thought.

"What makes you think you ever knew me, Raoul?" The elegant arches of her dark brows lifted while bitter amusement twisted her doll-perfect lips. "Did you ever ask about my life? My plans? My likes or dislikes? All I remember is demands that revolved around your needs. Your intention to work late. Your bad mood because you hadn't eaten. You once snapped your fingers at me because you wanted the name of the woman you'd taken to dinner, maybe even bed, the night before. She needed flowers as a kiss-off. On that note, as your former PA I'm compelled to point out that your new one dropped the ball. I didn't get my lilies."

Her audacity tested Raoul's already dicey mood. His inner compass swung from contempt to self-disgust that he'd slept with her at all to a guilty acknowledgment that no, he hadn't spent much time getting to know her on a personal level. He'd wanted too badly to take things to an intimate level, so he'd kept her at a distance.

Not that he had any intention of explaining when she was coming out swinging with two full buckets of scathing judgment and brutal sarcasm.

"That ice water seems to have gone directly into your veins," he remarked with the smoothness of a panther batting a bird from the air.

"Yes, I'm a kettle and so much blacker than you." She pivoted the file and pushed it toward him. "You might as well read my notes and we'll go from there."

Cold. Distant. Unreachable. She wasn't saying those words, but he'd heard them from enough women to know that's what she was implying.

Oddly, he hadn't thought Sirena saw him that way, and it bothered him that she did. Which made no sense, because he hadn't cared much when those other women said it and he hadn't once put Sirena in the same category as his former lovers. She was never intended to be his lover at all. When he took women to his bed, it was without any sort of expectation beyond an affair that would allow him to release sexual tension. Sirena had already been too integral a part of his working life to blur those lines.

Yet he had. And she seemed to be holding him to account for his callous treatment of her—when she had only slept with him for her own gain! Possibly for the very baby they were fighting over.

Drawing the papers closer, he began taking in her notations. The first was a refusal to submit to paternity tests until after the birth, at which point this contract would come into effect if he was proven to be the father.

He didn't like it, but in the interest of moving forward he initialed it.

Things quickly became more confusing and audacious. Distantly he noted that she'd circled a formatting error— one more eagle-eyed skill he regretted losing from his business life.

"Why the hell is everything to be held in trust for the baby?"

"I don't want your money," she said with such flatness he almost believed her.

Don't get sidetracked, he warned himself. Obviously she had wanted his money or she wouldn't have stolen from him, but arguing that point was moot. Right now all that mattered was getting paternity resolved and his right to involvement irrevocable.

He lowered his gaze to the pages in front of him, trying to make sense of her changes when they all favored the baby's financial future and left her taking nothing from him. Raoul cut her a suspicious glance. No one gave up this much…

"Ah," he snorted with understanding as he came to the codicil. *"No."*

"Think about it. You can't breast-feed. It makes sense that I have full custody."

"For *five* years? Nice try. Five days, maybe."

"Five days," she repeated through her teeth, flashing an angry emotion he'd never seen in her. Her eyes glazed with a level of hatred that pierced through his shell with unexpected toxicity, leaving a fiery sting.

And was that fear? Her generous mouth trembled before she pressed it into a firm line. "If you're not going to be reasonable, leave now. You're not the father anyway."

She rose and so did he, catching her by the arms as she tried to skirt past him. The little swell at her belly nudged into him, foreign and disconcerting, making his hands tighten with a possessive desire to keep her close. Keep *it* close, he corrected silently.

"Don't touch me." Fine trembles cascaded through her so he felt it as if he grasped an electric wire that pulsed in warning.

"Sure you don't want to try persuading me into clemency again?" he prodded, recognizing that deep down he was still weakly enthralled by her. If she offered herself right now, he would be receptive. It would change things.

"I didn't sue you for sexual harassment before, but I had every right to."

Her words slapped him. Hard.

Dropping his hold, he reared back, offended to his core. "You wanted me every bit as much as I wanted you," he seethed. His memories exploded daily with the way her expression had shone with excitement. The way she'd molded herself into him and arched for more contact and cried out with joy as the shudders of culmination racked them both.

"No, you were *bored*," she shot back with vicious fury that carried a ring of hurt.

It shouldn't singe him with guilt, but it did. He'd been saving face when he'd said that, full of whiskey and brimming with betrayal. The news that she had been released had been roiling in him like poison. Having her show up at the end of his drive had nearly undone him.

Now he teetered between a dangerous admission of attraction and delivering his brutal set-down for a second time.

"Get out, Raoul," Sirena said with a pained lack of heat. She sounded defeated. Heartbroken. "I'm sorry I ever met you."

The retort that the feeling was mutual hovered on his tongue, but stayed locked behind teeth clenched against a surprising lash of...hell, why would he suffer regret?

Pinching the bridge of his nose, he reminded himself the woman he'd thought he'd known had never existed. He threw himself back into his chair. "We'll hire a panel of experts to work out the schedule of the baby's first five years based on his or her personal needs. At four years we'll begin negotiating the school years."

"A panel of experts," she repeated on a choking laugh. "Yes, I've got your deep pockets. Let's do that."

"If you're worried about money, why are you refusing a settlement?"

Her response was quiet and somber, disturbingly sincere. "Because I don't want money. I want my baby." She moved to the window. It was covered in drizzle that the wind had tossed against the glass. Her hand rested on her belly. Her profile was grave.

Raoul dragged his eyes off her, disturbed by how much her earnest simplicity wrenched his gut. It made him twitch with the impulse to reassure her, and not just verbally. For some reason, he wanted to hold her so badly his whole body ached.

That wasn't like him. He had his moments of being a softy when it came to his mother or stepsister. They were beloved and very much his responsibility even though they weren't as helpless these days as they'd once been. He still flinched with guilt when he remembered how he'd been living it up his first year of college, drinking and chasing girls, completely oblivious to what was happening at home. Then, despite how brutal and thoughtless his stepfather's gambling had been, the man's death had shattered the hearts of two people he cared for deeply. Faced with abject poverty, it had been easy for Raoul to feel nothing but animosity toward the dead man, but the unmitigated grief his mother and Miranda had suffered had been very real. He'd hated seeing them in pain. It had been sharply reminiscent of his agony after his father's suicide.

But as supportive as he'd tried to be while he took control and recovered their finances, he'd never been the touchy-feely sort who hugged and cuddled away their pain.

Why he craved to offer Sirena that sort of comfort boggled him.

Forcing himself to ignore the desire, he scanned the changes she'd made to the agreement, thinking that perhaps he was more self-involved than he'd realized since he had been focused this entire time on what the child meant to him, how his life would change, how he'd make room for it and provide for *his* progeny. What *he* wanted.

Suddenly he was seeing and hearing what Sirena wanted and it wasn't to hurt him. She had ample ways to do that, but her changes to this document were more about keeping the baby with her than keeping it from him.

"Did you think about termination at all?" he asked with sudden curiosity.

"Yes."

The word struck him like a bullet, utterly unexpected and so lethal it stopped his heart. Until his mind caught up. Obviously she'd decided to have the baby or they wouldn't be here.

He rubbed feeling back into his face, but his ears felt filled with water. He had to strain to hear her as she quietly continued.

"I was only a few weeks along when I found out. There's a pill you can take that early. You don't have to go into hospital, there are fewer complications… There seemed to be a lot of good reasons not to go through with the pregnancy." Her profile grew distressed and her fingertips grazed the pulse in her throat.

Reasons like the threat of prison and having a man she didn't want in her life demanding access to her baby. Raoul's sharp mind pinned up the drawbacks as quickly as her own must have. His blood ran cold at how close he'd come to not knowing about this baby at all.

"I couldn't bring myself to…expel it from my life like that. I want this baby, Raoul." She turned with her hand protectively on her middle again, her eyes glittering with quiet ferocity. "I know it's foolish to let you see how badly I want it. You'll find a way to use it against me. But I need you to believe me. I will *never* let anyone take my baby from me."

His scalp tightened with preternatural wariness and pride and awe. Sirena was revealing the sort of primal mother instinct their caveman ancestors would have prized in a mate. The alpha male in him exalted in seeing that quality emanating from the mother of his child.

While the cutthroat negotiator in him recognized a tough adversary.

"You're trying to convince me I can't buy you off," he summed up, trying not to let himself become too entranced by her seeming to possess redeeming qualities. She had fooled him once already.

"You can't. The only reason I'm speaking to you at all is to give my baby the same advantages its father might provide its future siblings, whether that's monetary or social standing or emotional support. Consider what those things might be as you work through the rest of that." She nodded at the contract and slipped into the powder room again.

Future siblings? Raoul's mind became an empty whiteboard as he bit back a remark that he hadn't expected *this* child; he certainly wasn't ready to contemplate more.

Three months later, Raoul was taking steps to ensure he was prepared for the birth, looking ahead to clear his calendar in six weeks. He rarely took time off and found even Christmas with his mother an endurance test of agitation to get back to work. Anticipation energized him for this vacation, though.

Because it was a new challenge? Or because he would see Sirena?

He shut down the thought. The baby was his sole interest. He was eager to find out the sex, know it was healthy and have final confirmation it was *his*.

Not that he had many doubts on any of that. True to their agreement, Sirena had sent him updates on the baby's progress. Nothing concerning her own, he had noted with vague dissatisfaction, but he expected he would be informed if there were problems. The second scan later in the pregnancy had not revealed an obvious male, so he'd assumed the baby was female and found himself taken with the vision of a daughter possessing dark curls and beguiling green eyes.

As for paternity, to his mind, the fact Sirena had signed made the baby his. The final test after the birth was a formality that would activate the arrangements, that was all.

But that was a month and a half from now and he had people to organize. People who were abuzz with the news that the driven head of their multinational software corporation was taking an extended absence.

Only a handful of his closest and most trusted subordinates knew the reason, and even they didn't know the mother's identity. The scandalous circumstances of his father's infidelity and suicide had made Raoul a circumspect man. Nothing about his involvement with Sirena, their affair, her being fired for embezzlement or her pregnancy was public knowledge. When people asked—and she'd made enough of an impression on associates and colleagues that many did—he only said she was no longer with the company.

Part of him continued to resent that loss, especially when the assistants he kept trying out turned out to be so *trying.* The highly recommended Ms. Poole entered the meeting with a worried pucker in her magic-marker brows.

"I said life or death, Ms. Poole," he reminded, clinging to patience.

"She's very insistent," the spindly woman said, bringing a mobile phone to him.

"Who?" He tamped down on asking, *Sirena?* Her tenacity was something he'd come to respect, if not always appreciate.

"Molly. About your agreement with Ms. Abbott."

He didn't know any Molly, but something preternatural set an unexpected boot heel on his chest, sharp and compressing, causing pressure to balloon out in radiant waves. Odd. There was no reason to believe this was bad news. Sirena hadn't contacted him directly since he'd left her looking wrung out and cross at her flat that day, neither of them particularly satisfied with the outcome of their negotiations, but possessing a binding document between them.

"Yes?" He took the phone in a hand that became nerveless and clumsy. As he stood and moved from the table, he was aware of the ripple of curiosity behind him. At the same time, despite everything that had passed between them, he experienced a flick of excitement. His mind conjured an image of Sirena in one of those knitted skirt-and-sweater sets she used to wear.

"Mr. Zesiger? I'm Sirena Abbott's midwife. She asked me to inform you that the baby is on its way."

"It's early," he protested.

"Yes, they had to induce—" She cut herself off.

He heard muffled words and held his breath as he strained to hear what was said.

She came back. "I've just been informed it will be an emergency cesarean."

"Where is she?" he demanded while apprehension wrapped around him like sandpaper, leaving him abraded and raw.

"I understood you were only to be informed and that a paternity test be ordered, not that you would attend—"

"Save me the phone calls to find her so I can come directly," he bit out.

A brief pause before she told him. "But the results won't be known for days."

"Tell her I'm on my way," he said, but she was already gone.

CHAPTER FOUR

A WOMAN MET him in the hospital reception area. She wore red glasses and a homespun pullover. Her ditch-water hair was in one thick plait, her expression grave.

"Raoul? Molly." She held out a hand and offered a tight smile. "Sirena told me I'd know you when I saw you. The baby is a girl. They've taken the samples and should have the results in a few days." Her manner was disconcertingly strained.

Because she didn't want to get his hopes up? The baby was here, the moment of truth at hand. He shouldn't be so stunned given the nature of the call or the time it had taken to fight traffic to get here, but the swiftness of the procedure surprised him. At the same time, he was aware of a gripping need to see the infant and *know* she was his.

A girl. He hadn't realized how much he wanted one. And safely delivered. The abruptness of the call and lack of details had unsettled him, but they were fine. Everything was fine.

"Good," he heard himself say, finally able to breathe. "I'm pleased to hear they came through all right." He gestured for her to lead the way, assuming she'd show him to their room.

Molly didn't move. "Premature babies always have certain hurdles, but the pediatrician is confident she'll prog-

ress as well as the best of them." She seemed to ponder
whether to say more.

"And Sirena?" he prompted. Some unknown source of
telepathy made him brace even as the question left him. A
kind of dread that was distant but gut-churningly familiar seeped into his bloodstream like poison, unwanted and
tensing him with refusal and denial before he even knew
what she would say.

Molly's eyes became liquid. "They're doing all they
can."

For a long moment nothing happened. No movement,
no sound, nothing. Then, from far off, he heard a torn inhale, like a last gasp of life.

No. Her words didn't even make sense. He suddenly
found himself bumping into a wall and put out a hand to
steady himself. "What *happened?*"

"I wondered if she had told you about her condition."
Molly moved closer. Her touch was a biting grasp on his
upper arm, surprisingly strong and necessary as he wondered if he'd stay on his feet. "It's been a risky pregnancy
from the start. High blood pressure, then early-onset pre-
eclampsia. She's been managing that condition these last
few weeks, trying to buy the baby more time. Today they
couldn't wait any longer without risking both their lives, so
the doctors induced. After she had a seizure, they stopped
the labor and took her for surgery. Now she's lost a lot of
blood. I'm sorry. I can see this is hard for you to hear."

Hard? All his strength was draining away, leaving him
cold and empty. Clammy with fear. Her life was about to
snap free of his and she *hadn't even told him.* She might
as well have swallowed a bottle of pills and left herself for
him to find when he got home from school. Suddenly he
was nine again, barely comprehending what he was seeing, unable to get a response out of the heavy body he was

shaking with all his might. Not there soon enough. Helpless to make this right.

"Why the hell didn't she *say something?*" he burst out,
furious that she'd given him no indication, no warning, just
left him tied to the tracks to be hit with a train.

Molly shook her head in bafflement. "Sirena didn't talk
about the custody agreement, but it's been my impression
things have been hostile."

So hostile she kept from him that her life was on the
line?

"I don't want her to *die!*" The word was foul and jagged
in his throat. He spoke from the very center of himself,
flashing a look at Molly that made her flinch. He couldn't
imagine what he looked like, but his world was screech-
ing to a halt and everything in it was whirling past him.

"No one does," she assured him in the guarded tone developed by people who dealt with victims. It was the same
prudent nonengagement with explosive emotions that the
social worker had used as she had steered his young self
from his father's body.

"Take me to her," he gritted out. A horrible avalanche
of fear like he'd never known crushed him. He wanted to
run shouting for her until he found her. This wasn't real.
It couldn't be.

"I can't. But—" She seemed to think twice, then gave
him a poignant smile. "Maybe they'll let us into the nursery."

He forced one foot in front of the other, walking as if
through a wall of thick, suffocating gelatin as he followed
Molly to the preemie clinic, ambivalence writhing like
a two-headed snake inside him. Was it his fault Sirena
hovered on the brink? Or another man's? He adamantly
wanted his child, but the idea that one life could cost another appalled him.

He came up to the tiny, nearly naked being in the incubator, her bottom covered in an oversized nappy, her hair hidden by a cap. Wires extended from her bare fragile body and her miniature Sirena mouth briefly pursed in a kiss.

He couldn't see anything of himself in her, but a startlingly deep need to gather and guard the infant welled in him. Pressing his icy hands to the warm glass, he silently begged the little girl to *hang on*. If this was all that would be left of Sirena…

He brutally refused to entertain such a thought, turning his mind to sending a deep imperative through the walls of the hospital to the unknown location of this baby's mother. *Hang on, Sirena. Hang on.*

Sirena had the worst hangover of her life. Her whole body hurt, her mouth was dry and nausea roiled in her stomach. In her daze, she moved her hand to her middle, where the solid shape of her baby was gone, replaced with bandages and a soft waistline.

A whimper of distress escaped her.

"Lucy is fine, Sirena." His voice was unsweetened cocoa, warm and comforting despite the bitter taint.

"Lucy?" she managed, blinking gritty eyes. The stark ceiling above her was white, the day painfully bright. Slowly the steel-gray of Raoul's gaze came into focus.

"Isn't that what you told Molly? That you wanted your daughter named for your mother, Lucille?"

You don't mind? she almost said, but wasn't sure where the paternity test was. When she had signed the consent forms, they'd told her the kind of proof he'd requested, the kind admissible in court, was a more complex test that would take several days. She wondered if waiting on that had been the only thing keeping him from whisking Lucy from this hospital before she woke.

She didn't ask. She could barely form words with what felt like a cotton-filled mouth. It took all her concentra-

tion to remain impassive. Seeing him gave her such a bi-
zarre sense of relief she wanted to burst into tears. She
reminded herself not to read anything into the shadow of
stubble on his jaw or the bruises of tiredness under his
eyes. The man was a machine when it came to work; he
could have been at the office late and dropped by on his
way to his penthouse.

Still, that scruff of light beard gave her a thrill. She'd
seen him like this many times and always experienced
this same ripple of attraction. The same desire to smooth
a hand over his rough cheek. He would be overworked yet
energized by whatever had piqued his ambition, his shirt
collar open, his sleeves rolled back and soon, a smile of
weary satisfaction.

But not today. Today he was sexily rumpled, but his
demeanor was antagonistic, making a shiver of apprehension sidle through her as he spoke in a rough growl. "You
should have told me you weren't well."

The harsh accusation in his tone was so sharp she
flinched. All she could think about were those harrow-
ing moments when they'd told her the baby had to come
out. Not for Lucy's sake, but her own. The fear in her had
been so great, she'd been on the verge of begging Raoul to
come to her. The Raoul she had once imagined him to be
anyway. He was so strong and capable and she'd instinctively known she'd feel safe if he was near.

He hated her, though. He wouldn't care. Like always,
she'd been on her own.

She'd gone through the induction and the beginning of
pains without anyone at her side, only calling Molly when
the nurse confirmed that yes, labor was properly started.
That was when she'd been required to notify Raoul. She
had been explaining that to Molly when something went
wrong.

She didn't even know what had happened. Having a

huge blank like that was frightening. His blaming her for not advising him it was a possibility added insult to injury, putting her on the defensive.

"Why would I tell you anything?" she challenged from her disadvantaged position, flat on the bed, tied down with wires, voice like a flake of yellowed onionskin. "You can't be happy I pulled through."

"You haven't yet," he said, snapping forward in a way that made her heart jump. He set his big hands on either side of her and leaned over her, promising reprisal despite her pathetic condition. "And don't ever accuse me of anything so ugly again."

Sirena tried to swallow and couldn't even feel her dry tongue against her arid lips. "Can I have some water?" she begged in a whispered plea. "Please? I'm so thirsty."

"I don't know if you're allowed to have anything," he said with a scowl, something avid and desperate flickering through his eyes before he bent with the sudden swoop of a hawk going for a kill.

His mouth covered hers for the briefest second. His damp tongue licked into the parched cavern of her mouth to moisten the dry membranes. The relief was incredible, the act surprising and intimate beyond measure.

"I'll tell the nurse you're awake." He walked out, leaving her speechless and tingling with the return of life to her entire body, mind dazed and wondering if she was still unconscious and hallucinating.

Sirena had thought nothing could make her melt so thoroughly as the vulnerable sight of her premature daughter. Then she began hearing the stories of Raoul learning to diaper and feed her. Raoul, who didn't even know for sure he was the father, had paced a path between Lucy and Sirena, talking unceasingly to Sirena when they had feared she would slip into a coma. He'd only gone home for a shower and sleep now that Sirena had woken, nearly seventy-two hours after the birth.

She told herself not to read it as a sign of caring. If Raoul was tending to Lucy, he was only stamping a claim while trying to prove Sirena was dispensable. To some extent she was. She quickly learned she could hold her baby, but she was too sick and weak for anything else. She was pumping her breasts, but only to keep her thin milk supply going while she waited for the cocktail of medications to leave her system. She couldn't feed Lucy or do anything else a mother ought to do.

Dejected, she was fretting over how useless she was as she headed back to bed the next morning, wiped out by the tiny act of brushing her teeth.

Raoul walked in on her attempt to scale the bed, finding her with one hip hitched on the edge, bare legs akimbo as she quickly tried to stay decent under her hospital gown.

Aside from faint shadows under his heavy eyes, he looked fantastic in casual pants and a striped shirt. He brought a wonderfully familiar scent with him, too. For a second she was back in the office welcoming her freshly shaved boss, sharing coffee with him as they discussed how they'd tackle the day.

He eyed her balefully, but that might have been a reaction to the ferocious scowl she threw at him. She hadn't been allowed coffee since early in the pregnancy and he was sipping from a travel mug tagged with a ProZess Software logo. He was a picture of everything she couldn't have.

"Why are you here?" she asked, struggling to use her severed stomach muscles to heft herself onto the bed.

He smoothly moved to her side, set down his coffee and helped her.

"I don't—" She stiffened in rejection, but he bundled her into his crisp shirt anyway. The press of his body heat through the fabric burned into her as he used a gentle embrace to lift her. His free hand caressed her bare, dangling leg, sliding it neatly under the sheet as he slid her into bed as if she weighed no more than a kitten.

Shaken, she drew the sheet up to her neck and glared at him.

He picked up his coffee and sipped, staring back with his poker face. "Your doctor said he'd have the paternity results when he did his rounds this morning."

Her heart left her body and ran down the hall to bar the door of the nursery.

She wasn't ready to face this. Last night had been full of sudden jerks to wakefulness that had left her panting and unable to calm herself from the nightmare that Raoul would disappear with their daughter.

That *he* would disappear from her life again.

Why did it matter whether he was in her life? She felt nothing but hatred and mistrust toward him, she reminded herself. But the weeks of not seeing him while she waited out her pregnancy had been the bleakest of her life, worse even than when her family had left for Australia.

Logic told her he wasn't worth these yearning feelings she still had, but she felt a rush of delight that he kept showing up. When he was in the room, the longing that gripped her during his absences eased and the dark shadows inside her receded.

She couldn't forget he was the enemy, though. And she was running out of defenses.

He must have seen her apprehension, because he drawled, "Scared? Why?" The question was like a throwing star, pointed on all sides and sticking deep. "Because I might be the father? Or because you know I am?"

The stealthy challenge circled her heart like a Spanish inquisitor, the knife blade out and audibly scraping the strop.

She noticed her hands were pleating the edge of the sheet into an accordion. What was the use in prevaricating? She licked her numb lips.

"Are you going to try to take her from me if you are?" she asked in a thin voice.

If? You bitch, he thought as the tension of not knowing stayed dialed high inside him. The last three days had been hellish as he'd grown more and more attached to that tiny tree frog of a girl while cautioning himself that she might belong to another man.

Just like her mother.

"I could have taken her a dozen times by now," he bit out. "I should have."

It wasn't completely true. The hospital had accommodated his visiting the baby, but only because he was the kind of man who didn't let up until he got what he wanted. They wouldn't have let him leave with her, though.

If Sirena believed he could have, however, great. He wanted to punish her for the limbo she'd kept him in.

Her hands went still and pale. All of her seemed to drain of color until she was practically translucent, her already wan face ashen. Fainting again? He shot out a hand to press her into the pillows against the raised head of the bed.

She tried to bat away his touch, but in slow motion, her tortured expression lifting long enough to let him glimpse the storm of emotions behind her tangled lashes and white lips: frustration at her weakness, a flinch of physical pain in her brow, defensiveness that he had the audacity to touch her and terror. Raw terror in the glimmering green of her eyes.

Rolling her head away, she swallowed, her fear so palpable the hair rose on the back of his neck.

Advantage to me, he thought, trying to shrug off the prickling feeling, but guilty self-disgust weighed in the pit of his stomach. All he could think about was the hours he'd spent right here, telling her how unfair it was for a child to grow up missing a parent. The questions Lucy would have, the empty wedge in the wholeness of her life, would affect the child forever.

Blood ties hadn't mattered at that point. He and Lucy had been linked by the prospect that she would suffer his pain—an unthinkable cruelty for an infant just starting her life. The whole time he'd been urging Sirena to pull through, he'd been mentally cataloging everything he knew about her, wanting to be Lucy's depository of information on her mother.

While all he'd heard in the back of his mind had been Sirena's scathing, *What makes you think you ever knew me, Raoul?*

His heart dipped. She wanted her baby. He knew that much. As he'd gleaned all the details of this pregnancy that had nearly killed her, he'd wondered about her feelings for the father. Did the lucky man even know how stalwartly determined she'd been to have his child?

If that man was him… His abdomen tensed around a ripple of something deep and moving, something he didn't want to acknowledge because it put him in her debt.

The specialist swept in, taking in the charged tension with a somber look. "Good morning. I know you've been waiting, Raoul. Let me put you at ease. You are Lucy's biological father."

Relief poured into him like blood returning after a constriction, filling him with confidence and pride in his daughter, the little scrap with such a determined life force.

No reaction from Sirena. She kept her face averted as though he and the doctor weren't even in the room.

"I don't have plans to take her from you," Raoul blurted. The impatient words left him before he realized they were on his tongue, leaving him irritated by how she weakened him with nothing but terrified silence.

She gave him a teary, disbelieving look that got his back up.

The physician distracted her, asking after her incision and leaving Raoul to face a cold, stony truth: he couldn't separate mother from daughter.

Her accusation when she'd woken yesterday that he would have wished her dead had made him so sick he hadn't had words. His own father's absence had been self-inflicted—he'd *left* Raoul and his mother—but it didn't make the idea of Sirena's baby accidentally being motherless any less horrific. Raoul wouldn't be able to live with himself if he was the instrument that divided a parent from a child.

"When can I take her home?" he heard Sirena ask the doctor.

An image flashed into Raoul's mind of her collapsing the way she had at the courthouse, but without anyone to catch her or the baby in her arms.

"You're not taking her to your flat," he stated bluntly, speaking on instinct from the appalled place that was very much aware of how ill and weak she was.

Sirena's gaze swung to his, persecuted and wild. "You just said—"

"I said I wasn't so low I'd steal your baby from you. But you're more than prepared to keep Lucy from me, aren't you?" That reality was very raw. "You're the one who steals, Sirena, not me."

A humiliated blush rolled into her aghast face.

The physician broke in with, "Let's get you and Lucy well first, then we'll talk about where she's going." It was a blatant effort to defuse their belligerent standoff.

The doctor departed a few minutes later, leaving Sirena trying to decide which was worse: having Raoul in the room, where his presence ratcheted her tension beyond bearing, or out of the room, where she didn't know what he was up to.

"The contract is in effect now," she reminded him in a mutter. "I'll adhere to it."

"Will you? Because you've done everything possible to keep me from even knowing she's mine." His temper snapped. "How could you do that? I lost my father, Sirena. I know how it feels to grow up without one."

"And I lost my mother," she cried, then cringed as the force of such harsh speech sliced pain across her abdomen. "Why do you think I stood up to the most pitiless man in the world?" she asked in a thick voice, clenching her eyes shut as she fought for control, so emotional from everything that she verged on breaking down. "You really know how to put a woman through hell, Raoul. I can't even get myself down the hall to her and you're playing stupid mind games. *I won't take her, but you can't have her.* Maybe you would deserve a place in her life if you just once showed an ounce of compassion."

Silence.

She threw her heavy arm over her closed eyes, pressing back weak tears, concentrating on her breathing to pull herself together. The worst part was, she felt horrible about trying to keep him from Lucy. He had a right to be angry about that—along with the stealing—but she couldn't undo any of it. Her life was a giant mess and she had no idea how she was going to fix it and carry on.

"Let's go," Raoul said in a gruff tone that was too close to the bed.

Sirena lowered her arm to eye him, startled to see he'd brought the wheelchair to her side.

"I'll take you to see Lucy. We'll both calm down and maybe start communicating like adults."

"Don't be nice," she groaned. "It makes me feel awful."

"You should feel awful." He braced her as she slid off the bed and into the chair.

She slumped into it and dropped her face into her hands. "I love her more than you can know, Raoul. And you've been horrid, trying to take her from me the instant you heard I was pregnant. What else could I do except lie about paternity?"

The chair moved and she lifted her head, glad she didn't have to face him, especially when he said with quiet sincerity, "You're wrong. I do know how much you love her. I feel the same way. That's why I've been so tough about it. I didn't know about your mother. I thought this was all payback for the court case."

"No," she breathed, shoulders slumping. "I'm angry about that, but—" her voice hitched with yearning "—I just want to be her mum."

"What happened to yours?" His voice sounded deeper and quieter than she'd ever heard it, making her feel small for trying to cut him from his daughter's life. She didn't know how he'd lost his father, but that nascent connection she'd always felt toward him over their shared grief extended from within herself, like a strand of spiderweb drifting behind her, searching to anchor itself to him.

"This." She waved a trembling hand at her pathetic physical state. "Her complications were different so this wasn't hereditary, but it was always in my mind that having a baby isn't as simple for some as it is for others. I was only six when she died, so I don't have a lot of memories, but that's why losing her hurt so much. I can't bear the idea of Lucy going through all her life markers of puberty and boyfriends and childbirth without her mother there for her."

He stayed silent behind her, giving no indication whether her words had any impact. She wasn't able to twist around and look and didn't want to anyway. He might be interpreting her confession as a plea for sympathy when it was the kind of opening of her heart that left her feeling so raw and exposed she could hardly bear it.

She was grateful they entered the quiet warmth of the nursery at that point. Seconds later, as she cuddled Lucy into her chest, her world righted, becoming achingly perfect, even with Raoul's commanding presence hovering over them. Maybe because he was here. Much as she resented him, she wanted Lucy to have her father.

After feeding and changing and getting an update on Lucy's progress, Raoul returned Sirena to her room. She was quiet, visibly exhausted, their silence no longer hostile. When he helped her into bed, she only murmured, "Thank you," before plummeting into sleep.

Such a ferocious scrapper and now he understood why. The way she'd talked about missing her mother had made something lurch in his chest. It was a renewed snag of guilt at not really knowing her. His resentful *I never dreamed she was capable of stealing* was shifting into *still waters run deep.*

The way his father had quit on him made him highly susceptible to exalting a woman who had fought so hard to give her child life and to be in it.

He didn't like this shift in him. It made him wonder about her motives for stealing, and he didn't want to develop compassion and forgiveness for that. Opportunists took advantage of weak emotions like affection and trust. Next thing you knew, you were on the streets with two dependents—a social pariah—and your path forward was a broken cliff into an abyss.

He couldn't doubt Sirena's love for their daughter, though. While in the nursery, the old Sirena had returned, all warm smiles and soft laughter, her expression open and her wit quick, making the nurses laugh. He'd had to bite back his own chuckle more than once, fighting a desire to let go of his defenses and fall under her spell again.

Scowling, he tried to imagine how this impossible situation would play out. A foolish idea was taking hold in the back of his mind, one that looked ridiculous as a thought bubble. It would be outrageous in real life. He needed distance, not more exposure to her, but they were both coming from the same place with regard to Lucy. He couldn't ignore that. In fact, as the days passed, it was *all* he could think about.

Their truce lasted through the week as Raoul spent most of the day with them. Sirena stopped using the chair and started breast-feeding, even brought Lucy into her room with her overnight, which was a struggle she tried not to reveal, fearful of winding up in a fight with Raoul that she didn't have the energy to win. The rapport between them might be guarded and impersonal, but it was safe. As long as she didn't give him anything to criticize, they got along fine.

Meanwhile, the reality of taking a baby back to her flat when she couldn't even properly care for herself ate at her. When her doctor cleared her for discharge, she should have been elated, but she was so overwhelmed she hardly contained her tears.

Of course Raoul arrived at that exact moment. He was wearing a suit and tie, the shoulders of his jacket speckled with damp spots of late-spring rain. No time to worry how she'd cope when she had bigger concerns confronting her from the foot of her hospital bed. Dark, handsome, vengeful concerns.

"I told you a week ago you I won't let you take her to your flat," he said unemotionally.

It was the fight she'd been dreading, but she still wasn't prepared for it.

"And I'm pretty sure we signed an agreement that said I could," she replied, trying not to let him stir her temper. "I have nights with Lucy. You can visit during the day, exactly as we're doing here. Are we ignoring the panel of experts you hired?" Her quick sarcasm was a show of strength she didn't have. She had just gotten back from walking down the hall and that snappy reply was the extent of the spunk in her.

"You have the stamina of a trampled daisy. What if something happened? No. You're coming home with me," Raoul pronounced.

For a few seconds, she couldn't even blink. A tiny voice deep in her soul asked, *Me? Not just Lucy?* Her pulse tripped into a gallop and tingling excitement raced all the way to her nerve endings.

Get a grip, Sirena!

"I have staples, Raoul. It's not nice to make me laugh," she retorted, trying to gather thoughts that had scattered like shards of glass from a broken window. Stay in his house? With him? She already felt too vulnerable seeing him during the day. Living off him would decimate her pride and put her in his debt.

"You do," Raoul agreed with edgy derision. "Staples and tubes and a unit of someone else's blood. You're on medications that make you light-headed and have appointments for follow-up and a baby to care for. You can't do it alone."

In her heart of hearts she'd been counting on a miracle with her sister, but of course that hadn't panned out. Her father wasn't working, so he couldn't foot the bill for plane fare and God knew she couldn't afford it. Besides, Ali was in her first semester at uni—that had been the whole point of Sirena sending the money so many months ago.

Sirena had friends she could call for the odd thing, but

not the sort of steady help she needed these first weeks at home. Frustration made her voice strident.

"Why would you even suggest it? You don't want anything to do with me," she accused, voicing the fear that was a dark plague inside her.

He tilted his arrogant head to a condescending angle. "You may not be my ideal choice as the mother of my child, but I can't overlook the fact that you are, or that you love her as much as I do. We both want to be with her and you need looking after. Bringing you into my home is clearly the most practical solution."

That uncouched *not be my ideal* stung like mad. She knew she looked awful, hair flat and dull, no makeup. Her figure would remain a disaster until she could start on the treadmill again.

Was he seeing anyone, she wondered suddenly? It was the sort of thing she hadn't been able to avoid knowing when she'd been working for him—and bizarrely, after being fired she'd found the not knowing even worse. How would she feel to learn he was with another woman while she was sleeping under his roof?

She broke their locked gazes, deeply repelled by the idea of him in bed with other women. "We don't even like each other. It would be a disaster."

"We're going to have to get past that for Lucy's sake, aren't we?" he countered.

"And my being dependent on you will foster goodwill? I doubt it," she argued, even as she mentally leaped to the pro of still being able to do her transcription jobs if he was on hand to care for Lucy for an hour here and there. That would mean she could keep her flat. The prospect of losing her home had become a genuine concern.

Raoul folded his arms as he put his sharp mind to work finding the argument that would clinch what he wanted.

Not that he *wanted* her in his home, he reminded himself. It was his daughter he was after.

"If I were to have another child, I would look after the health of that child's mother. Didn't you tell me you expect me to offer Lucy the same considerations I would offer all my children?"

He was pleased to recall the demand she'd thrown at him weeks ago. It justified taking her into his home. He didn't need a volatile mix of leftover attraction and betrayal confronting him with his eggs every morning, but Lucy's needs trumped his.

Sirena heard the logic, but couldn't bring herself to acknowledge it. His dispassionate reasoning was exactly that: lacking in feeling, practical. Cold.

It was also a perfect out, allowing her to accept a crazy arrangement for sensible reasons, but she feared she was only giving in to temptation. She knew why, too. Deep down, a grossly foolish part of herself believed that if she could just have his attention long enough, she could explain and earn his forgiveness.

The loss of his good opinion crushed her, not abating despite the months that had passed since the lawsuit. Experience with her stepmother told her that imagining she could earn Raoul's admiration was pure self-delusion, but that didn't alter the fact that she desperately wanted him to stop hating her.

While he wanted unfettered access to his daughter. That's all that motivated him and he was trying to make it happen with his typical brook-no-arguments leadership and infinite resources, standing there casually impeccable and vaguely bored, certain he had the entire thing sewn up.

"Did I ever tell you how annoyingly bigheaded you can be when you think you've had the last word?" she muttered while casting for a suitable reason to refuse.

"I don't *think* I've had it, I know it. The doctor won't release you unless you have a care plan in place. I'm it."

"You're my get-out-of-jail card? When you put it like that…"

Every muscle in his body seemed to harden. "Be careful, Sirena. I'm taking into account you're still only half-alive. Once you're back to full strength, I won't be nearly so charitable. I've forgotten nothing."

A futile yearning swelled in her chest and burned in the back of her throat. He had every right to be angry, but to have her arrested when she'd been like an appendage for him for two years, then had given herself to him without hesitation…?

"You know I can't have sex for another five weeks, right?" she threw at him. "If you're thinking to have a convenient outlet on hand, it won't happen."

He swept her with one pithy glance that reminded her she was far beneath her best. She hated both of them in that second. Why did she care whether he was attracted to her or ever had been? He hadn't. He'd been horny and she'd been handy. He'd told her so. Apparently having her underfoot wouldn't be handy enough to tempt him again. That should be a comfort, not a knife in the heart.

"Just until the doctor clears me to live alone," she muttered, bolstering her humiliated blush with a level glance into his implacable face. "I'm only staying until I'm back to full strength. Then Lucy comes to my flat with me."

"We'll burn that bridge when we get to it."

Despite the welcome of blooming gardens at the house in Ascot, Sirena was icy cold as they drove past the gates where she'd stood waiting for Raoul in the rain, begging him over the intercom to speak to her.

Finding him here that day had been a matter of calling in a favor with an out-of-the-know workmate. After that she'd been shut out completely, her personal items from her desk returned and her keys, company ID, equipment and expense cards taken back.

Unable to look at him, she set a light hand on the warm shape of the baby between them and rocked numbly with the car when the chauffeur halted under the portico. As she reached to unclip the child seat, Raoul's adept fingers brushed hers away.

"I'll bring her." He relayed the diaper bag to his chauffeur and lifted Lucy out the opposite door, coming around to meet Sirena where the chauffeur had opened her door.

She tried to climb from the low-slung car and was more resentful than grateful when Raoul reached to help, offering his arm so she could cling to it with a shaky grip. Her muscles burned at the strain of pulling up and steadying herself on her weak legs. Pain sliced across her middle where her incision was healing.

As they went up the steps, he slipped his arm around her and half carried her.

She made a noise of protest, but couldn't help leaning into his support, both bolstered and weakened by his lean hardness. She finally gave in to the pull of attraction and let her head loll into his shoulder for just a second before he spoke, his tone flatly shoving her back to reality.

"You shouldn't have been discharged."

"I don't want to be this feeble," she grumbled, pulling away as they crossed the threshold. The loss of his touch made her feel weak and sorry for herself. "Even that time in Peru I managed to keep going. I'll get better. I have to." She sank down on the velvet-upholstered bench in the foyer and cupped her swimming head in her hands.

"When were you sick in Peru? That time half the conference came down with food poisoning? You didn't get it."

"I did! But someone had to take charge, extend the arrangements with the hotel and rebook the flights. I didn't hear you volunteering."

He grew an inch in height and his mouth opened, but she waved a hand against whatever scathing response he was on the verge of making.

"It was my job. I'm not complaining, just saying that's the most wretched and useless I've ever felt, but this is worse. I hate being like this."

"You should have told me. This time *and* then."

"It was my job," she repeated, ignoring his admonition in favor of reminding him her work ethic had been rock solid. She looked up at him and he met her gaze with an inscrutable frown and a tic in his cheek.

"I expect you to tell me what your needs are, Sirena. I'm not a mind reader. We'll go to your room now so you can rest. Can you manage these stairs with me or shall I have a room prepared down here?"

"Upstairs is fine, but Lucy will need a feed before I lie down." She deliberately kept her gaze on the baby and not on these beloved surroundings. Silly, naive fool that she was, she used to host fantasies about one day being mistress here. She loved everything about its eclectic style.

The lounge where she moved to nurse was one of her favorite rooms, with its Mediterranean colors, contemporary furniture and view to the English garden. Raoul had a lot of worldly influences in his life, from his Spanish mother's ancestry of warmth and sensuality to his father's Swiss precision. He had been educated in America, so he brought those modern, pop-culture elements into his world with contemporary art and futuristic electronics. All of his homes were classy, comfortable and convenient.

And all contained the one ingredient to which she was drawn inexorably: him.

He stood in profile to her, lean and pantherish, thumb sweeping across the screen of his mobile as he dealt with all the things she used to do for him. Her heart panged. She had loved working for him, loved the job that challenged her. Transcribing had put her through business school and kept her fed these last months, so she couldn't knock it, but it didn't take her off her steno chair, let alone around the world.

"Are you going in to the office this afternoon?" she asked, of two minds whether she wanted him to leave. Being on guard against him drained her, but another secret part of her drank up his nearness like a cactus in a rare rain.

"They're asking the same. Things are in disarray. When you delivered, I had only starting to put things in place for an absence I thought would happen next month."

"I'm sorry," she said, feeling the habitual words leave her lips and thinking, *Why are you apologizing? It's not your fault!*

"A warning that premature delivery was a possibility would have been helpful."

The supercilious remark got her back up. "I didn't need the extra stress of you hanging over me telling me what to do," she said with acerbity. "I followed doctor's orders and tried to go to term, which is all I *could* do. If you're inconvenienced by the early birth, well, welcome to parenthood. I believe we're both in for adjustments."

"A little communication goes a long way, is what I'm saying. Keeping things to yourself is a theme that keeps getting you into trouble." His deceptively silky tone rang with danger.

"Oh, and you gave me ample opportunity to communicate after informing me *through the arrest charges* that you knew money had gone missing?"

"Before that," he snapped. His jaw was like iron, his gray eyes metallic and locked down, but he did darken a shade with something that might have been culpability.

"You could have told me you were having financial troubles and we could have worked something out. Stealing from me was unacceptable."

"I agree. That's why I only borrowed."

"So you've said," he ground through his teeth. "But if you—"

Lucy made a little sputter. Sirena quickly sat her up, glancing at Raoul to finish his sentence, but he had stopped speaking to stare openly at her nude breast. She'd come to the demoralizing realization that there was no dignity in childbirth and there wasn't much more afterward. You needed two hands on a newborn, leaving none for tucking yourself back into a bra that had more jibs and sails than a yacht.

"You burp her," she ordered out of self-conscious embarrassment, screening herself with an elbow and quickly covering up once he'd taken the baby. It was an awkward moment on the heels of a deeper fight that promised her stay here would be a dark corner of hell.

When he helped her up the stairs a few minutes later, draped a coverlet over her and set a baby monitor on the nightstand, tears nearly overwhelmed her. A confusion of gratitude and relief with a hefty dose of frustration and fear of the unknown filled her. This wasn't the way she'd expected her life would turn out and she didn't know which way it would bend next. She couldn't trust Raoul, but she had to, at least for an hour while her body recovered enough to take him on next round.

Struggling to keep her heavy eyelids open, she said, "I didn't look to see which room you're putting her in. I won't know where to go if I hear her."

With a sardonic quirk of his mouth, he said, "The monitor is so I can hear you. I have a cot in my office for Lucy."

She really did want to cry then. He was the capable one and she would never measure up. She closed her eyes against the sting and clamped her trembling lips together, praying he couldn't tell how vulnerable she was.

Sirena fell asleep like a blanket had been dropped over her.

Raoul frowned, wanting to set a hand alongside her face to check for temperature, but he didn't want to disturb her. She needed the rest too badly.

Yet she insisted on wearing herself out by fighting him at every turn. What would she be like full strength? He kept seeing glimpses of the old Sirena in her sharp wit, but the hostility and challenges were new and disconcerting. How much of her real personality had she repressed while she had worked for him because he was the boss and she the employee?

And because she had wanted to lull him into not missing stolen money?

He scowled. That act didn't fit with the woman who had pushed herself to work when she was sick. Or pushed herself through a difficult pregnancy to give the best start in life to a baby whose birth could have killed her.

The sight of Sirena unconscious and white, tubes and wires keeping her alive, would never leave him. For that act alone, he owed her consideration. A chance to recover, at least.

Her obvious love for their daughter played on him too. Her worry after each medical checkup. The way she looked to him for his interpretation and reassurance. A cynical part of him warned against being taken in again, but her connection to their baby was too real to be manufactured.

Then there was the sexual attraction that was as bad as ever, despite how pale and weak she was. He hadn't been able to stop himself ogling her naked breast. Her ass was gorgeously round and begging to be fondled. Every time he got near enough to catch her scent, he wanted to pull her close and kiss the hell out of her plump, smart mouth.

He rubbed his face, more preoccupied than ever by a woman he never should have touched. Work was what he needed. Studying had been his escape from the struggle to understand his father's suicide. From age twenty, once his stepfather's perfidy came to light, he'd been immersed in recovering their finances. The urgency of that task had been a type of salvation from emotional angst as well.

Thankfully, despite having to drop out of university, he'd had a basic version of a software program more than halfway through development. Taking it to completion and selling it had staved off his sense of failure over not realizing what his stepfather had been doing. Piling up dollars and assets like points on a screen ever since had become enormously satisfying. It always reassured him to know he was creating not just a financial umbrella, but a giant, inflated mattress of protection for his family.

A family that now included a helpless infant. That gave him more motivation than ever.

And that baby's mother?

He took his seat at his desk and angled the baby monitor, staring hard at it until he heard her whispery breath, wondering where Sirena would fit into his life long-term.

CHAPTER FIVE

IN SOME WAYS, living with Raoul was too easy. The subliminal communication they had developed working together laid the groundwork. She knew his moods, picked up the small cues that meant his call would be a long one and already knew his boundaries when it came to making a space for her within his. Plus, he was such a work hound she was able to sneak away to quiet corners until he took a breather and came looking for his daughter.

But being out of his sight didn't mean he was out of her mind. Why, oh, why did she have to track him with internal radar, her entire being called by his dynamic presence? No matter how many times she told herself to get over him, knowing how close he was made her mind trail back to a rainy afternoon's passionate coming together. So stupid! Daydreams like that made her a pushover for what had been an impersonal coupling on his part. It's what had gotten her into this mess.

She should move back to her flat, but that circumstance was being influenced by other ones, putting a pleat in her brow.

"Was that the doctor?" he asked, startling her with a jolt of unexpected excitement because she had been certain he was in his office down the hall.

Trying to downplay the way she exploded with joyful awareness, she walked the cordless phone across the lounge to return it to its cradle.

"Indra. My neighbor." Her skin tingled despite her internal willing of the heat to leave her cheeks. These encounters in lounges and dining rooms were unbearable.

"Did something happen? You're frowning."

Don't study me, she wanted to cry. Never had she imagined she would long to go back to when she'd been one more piece of equipment in his high-tech office, but his aloof attitude had been a lot easier to deal with. Nowadays he watched her every move as though trying to read between her lines and catch her in a lie.

"Everything is fine," she said with false nonchalance. "She was asking how long I'd be out of my flat. We always had an arrangement when I was traveling that if she had family staying, they could use my place. Her niece is arriving with her new husband and, not surprisingly, they would love the privacy."

Awkward sexual awareness poured through her in an infuriating blush. She hadn't been cleared for sex and Raoul had made it plain he wasn't interested. Talking about intimacy shouldn't cause her to simmer with responsiveness, but she became enormously conscious of his masculine silhouette—so wide across the shoulders and narrowing down to those powerful thighs. She desperately wished she could swallow back her reference to the intimate things that happened between a man and a woman.

While Raoul flicked a glance down the T-shirt and yoga pants that were snug on her still-plump body. "What did you tell her?" he asked, his voice so devoid of any hint as to his thoughts she only felt more ill at ease and anxious to disappear.

"That I wished I could help her, but I'll need it sooner rather than later." There. She'd drawn the line.

He met her stare with one equally as steady. "What has the doctor said?"

"Stay out of the pool for another week but short walks are fine. Sleep." She gave him a dry look. "Apparently he's unaware that babies are night creatures."

He frowned. "Why didn't you say? I can get up with Lucy."

"What's the point? You don't have functioning breasts." Again with the dirty talk. Now all she could think of was his naked, very masculine chest, layered with muscle and sprinkled with fine, springy hairs. *Stop!* She turned to hide her flaming face.

"I can change her and settle her back to sleep as well as you can," he pointed out.

She tensed. He was proving himself to be the generous, involved parent she had known he would be, but after so many years without any sort of support, it was ingrained in her to do things by herself.

"I need to manage on my own," she dismissed. "Soon I'll have no choice. And you're working. You need your sleep."

"What do you call transcribing?" he asked with the irritated tone he'd taken the first time he'd found her at it. "You're courting a setback, pushing yourself like that." He spoke in the lofty way that made him a confident company president and a completely annoying adversary.

"I'm not overdoing it. My recovery is my priority. I know my freedom with Lucy hinges on it." She flashed a meaningless smile. "Don't worry. I won't be underfoot any longer than necessary."

That didn't seem to reassure him. His frown deepened. Fortunately Lucy woke and Sirena had a reason to escape the intensity of his inscrutable presence.

Raoul's perfectly functioning libido watched Sirena's curvy behind zip from the room. He was highly attuned

to the meaning behind sudden blushes and flustered dis-
appearing acts. They were the kind of signals that pro-
voked any man's interest and he was already interested.
Way too interested.

Back when he'd first hired Sirena, he'd seen the same
little betrayals of attraction. It hadn't meant anything to
him, since women always reacted to him. He had money,
worked out, dressed well and groomed daily. Sirena's sup-
pressed awareness had been routine.

He'd ignored it and his own sexual curiosity right up
until That Day. Since then, she'd been spitting and hissing
and so washed-out he'd felt like a lecher for any less than
pure thoughts. Today, however, her nervously smoothing
her hair and standing straighter while seeming ultraper-
turbed by her aroused senses was insanely seductive.

Emphasis on *insane*. So what if her body was recovered
enough to feel a flash of chemistry? He couldn't act on it.
They were barely capable of civility. Sex would make an
already complicated relationship completely unworkable.

It would be easier on his libido if she left, he acknowledged grudgingly. Her involuntary reaction had pulsed
male arousal through him so strongly he was drawn taut,
his erection thrusting against the confines of his pants,
throbbing with imperative to hunt down the woman who
had incited him and find relief in the wet depths that had
welcomed him deliciously almost a year ago.

There was the problem. It had been a year, he dismissed,
trying to forget the whole thing.

He remained edgy into the late hours, though, even
after he had accounted for his long spell of abstinence
with time spent at work and with lawyers. He'd been too
busy to date. It wasn't that he was so bewitched by one
particular woman that only she would do.

Hell. He should visit the city and exercise his urges.

Yes, that was the solution. He loathed the idea of Lucy moving out, so—

He paused in dousing his bedroom light, hearing Lucy start crying again. Sirena kept telling him the nights were hers, but this was silly. They shared parenting well enough through the daylight hours. She was being stubborn to prove a point that was totally lost on him.

By the time he moved down the darkened hall, Lucy was quiet again and Sirena was gently closing the nursery door. She jumped as his shadow joined hers on the wall, gasping as she swung around to confront him.

Clutching her heart, she scolded in a whisper, "You scared me to death!"

"I live here," he drawled, not the least bit scared even though his heart began to pound. She stood eye level to his naked chest, her bewildered expression burnished gold by the night-light. She was braless under a sleeveless tank and a pair of loose shorts that looked like men's boxers, her nipples sharply peaked against light cotton.

Damn. This was the wrong kind of night sharing, but he couldn't stop the bombardment of erotic signals that plowed into his sexual receptors. Her hair was loose and wavy. She was lightly scented from the bubble bath she'd taken earlier. Her breath hitched behind invitingly parted lips while her hungry gaze swept across his pecs, stinging him like licks from a velvet whip.

He wore loose pajama pants that drew a relaxed line across his flat abdomen, but they began to tent—

She yanked her gaze to his, embarrassed and deeply apprehensive.

And, if he wasn't mistaken, as dazed with repressed sexual need as he was.

"It didn't sound like she was settling," he managed gruffly, recalling why he was here. "I was coming to take over so you could go back to bed." *Bed*. It was all he could think about. They'd used a sofa that other time and for less than an hour. He wanted more. Hours. Days.

Raoul's voice made the hairs stand up all over her body. His scent was charged and aggressive, as though he hadn't quite made it to bed yet, while she was sleepy and befuddled. She became screamingly aware that her hair was everywhere and her thin tank and loose shorts weren't exactly sexy lingerie. That was probably a good thing, but she secretly wished she looked attractive.

Idiot.

"She's sleeping now," she mumbled and sidestepped at the same time he did, almost coming up against him as he loomed before her.

It was the foyer in Oxshott again. Her startled gaze came up in time to see his focus drop to her mouth. Her heart soared and her mind blanked, just like last time.

Not again, she thought, but couldn't move, paralyzed by attraction and wonder.

His hand came up and hesitated. The bare skin of her shoulder waited, nerve endings reaching out in anticipation. Raoul started to bend his head.

Don't let it happen, she warned herself with anxious intensity, but her self-preservation instincts were flash-firing so rapidly she couldn't figure out if she should retreat the wrong way down the hall, barrel through him or exit into Lucy's room.

His big hand cradled the side of her face, tilting her mouth up to his as his mouth crashed down on hers on an aggrieved groan.

Don't— Oh, do...

Everything about him was strong and the way his mouth covered hers, so confident and hungry, overcame her willpower. The shape of his lips fit hers perfectly. When the tip of his tongue parted her lips, she shuddered in renewal. *Oh, please.* She melted into him. She couldn't help it. She knew how good it could be between them. Her body remembered the virile feel of his muscles gathering, the fullness of him inside her...

His forearm angled across her back with proprietary strength, tugging her into a soft collision that made her release a throaty cry that he swallowed. Their nightclothes were no shield. She felt *everything.* The hot roughness of his chest, the flat muscles of his waist under confused hands that didn't know where to land and the fierce shape of his supremely eager erection.

Her hands splayed on his smooth waist while her thoughts receded behind a kiss that began to consume her. Sweet, deep arousal, a sensation she hadn't felt in months, twined through her, coiling deliciously. It felt so good to be held. The way his breath hissed and he plundered her mouth as though he was slaking a lifetime of need caught her as nothing else could, making her strain to match his voracious desire.

As his hands slid over her shape, she wriggled and pressed into his touch, reveling in the way he shifted her into the hard plane of the door so he could sandwich her with his weight. When his hot hand rode up her bare thigh under the leg of her shorts and found no underpants, he groaned and nipped a line down her neck while his flat hand shaped the globe of her bottom, squeezed gently, massaged and claimed.

She arched her breasts into his chest and her hands went to where his rampant stiffness was nearly piercing a hole through the light silk of his pants.

"Yes, touch me," he said raggedly and bared himself, wrapping his hand over hers with a crushing grip. His mouth came back to catch her cry of surprise while his own hand went up the front of her thigh, fingertips unerringly finding her plump, aching center and drawing a line into the wet slickness. The circling touch of his fingertip against the tight knot of nerves struck bolts of need into her core, driving her to push against his touch, squeeze him tight, kiss him with complete abandon.

He bared her breast and bent his head. She thought, *I'm nursing.*

The reality of what they were doing crashed into her. She shoved him back a step, dislodging his touch, making him stagger and lift his head.

There were so many reasons to be aghast. Her appalled fear must have shown on her face. His glazed eyes met hers and he drew in a breath of shock.

Maybe he was equally horrified to see whom he'd accidentally fallen into kissing.

Just the nearest woman. The one who was *handy.*

Hurt knifed into her abdomen, twisting painfully. Freshly humiliated, Sirena elbowed past him and fled to her room.

She slept late. That beastly man had sneaked into her room after she fell asleep and stolen the baby monitor. He was at the breakfast table when he should have been in his office. Why he wasn't going into the city to work escaped her. It had been nearly a month since he'd had a full day there.

"Lucy?" she prompted, looking past him.

"I gave her a bottle, but she didn't take much. She's down, but probably not for long."

At least that gave her an excuse to avoid him while she disappeared to pump the ache out of her swollen breasts. He was still at the table when she returned. He wore his I've-got-all-day-so-don't-bother-stalling face.

"I don't want to talk about it," she said flatly, veering her gaze from the way his muscled shoulders filled his ice-blue shirt. If only she wasn't so hungry. She folded a leg under her as she took a seat and reached for a piece of cold, buttered toast, biting into it mutinously.

He set aside his tablet and leaned his forearms where his place setting had been cleared.

"I know you can't make love yet. I wouldn't have taken it that far. I didn't have protection either and I sure as hell don't want to get you pregnant again."

The bite of toast in her mouth turned coarse and bitter. All the hurt she'd been bottling and ignoring rose in the back of her throat to make swallowing difficult. She rose up from her chair with what she hoped was enough indignation to cover her wounded core.

"Do you think I don't wish every day that Lucy's father was anyone but you?" She heard the cut of his breath and knew she'd scored a direct hit, but there was no satisfaction in it. She had zero desire to stick around and gloat.

She was almost to the door when he said with sharp force, "Because I don't want to risk your life again. Given how dangerous I've learned childbirth can be, I don't intend to put any woman through that ever again."

The statement was shocking enough to make her hesitate. She glanced back, certain he couldn't be as serious as he sounded. His still posture and set jaw told her he was incontrovertibly sincere.

"Millions of women sail through pregnancy and deliver without any trouble," she pointed out. "You don't know how you'll feel in future, with a different woman."

He only gave her that shuttered look that told her any sort of discussion on the matter was firmly closed. She was wasting her breath if she thought she could reason with him. His rigid expression was so familiar, his certainty that he was right so ingrained and obvious, she felt her lips twitch in amusement.

It was the last reaction she expected. Her body was still humming with unsatisfied arousal, which only increased her aggravation and trampled self-worth. Her heart had shriveled overnight into a self-protective ball, but for some reason his misplaced, oddly gallant statement uncurled it a bit. He was showing the protectiveness she so admired in him, and it was directed at her. Well, all women, maybe, but it still felt kind and yes, there was even a weak part of her that took comfort in knowing he wasn't likely to fill his life with children by other women. The thought of him making babies with someone he actually loved had been quietly torturing her.

"What's funny?" he demanded.

"Nothing," she assured him, pressing a hand to her hollow stomach as it growled.

He rose with impatience to hold her chair. "Sit. Eat. You need the calories."

She returned to slide into her chair as his housekeeper brought a plate of eggs and tomato.

To her consternation, Raoul sat down again.

The memory of last night blistered her as the housekeeper left them alone. She had tossed and turned after their rendezvous, trying to figure out how it had happened. For her it was simple: she still reacted to him. For him... convenience? It had to be. He wasn't going into the city to work *or* to work out his kinks.

Blushing with anger and remembered excitement, she stared at her plate, picking at her food with the tines of her fork. That wild moment was going to sit between them like the wall of resentment over the missing money, filling all of their interactions with undercurrents. She needed her own space.

"I should be able to move into my flat after my next appointment," she said.

He made a noise of negation.

She set her chin to disguise the leap in her heart. She was still processing that he hadn't actually insulted the hell out of her a few minutes ago. Was he resisting her leaving because he wanted her here?

Pressing her knotted fists into her lap, she asked, "Sooner, then?"

"Never. I want Lucy full-time. That means you have to stay, too."

The words went through her like a bomb blast, practically lifting the hair off her head and leaving her ears ringing. Unexpected yearning clenched in her and last night's excitement flared like stirred coals reaching toward a conflagration. Warning bells in her head clanged *danger, danger.*

"There you go testing my incision again," she said, and scooped eggs into her mouth as though the matter was closed. It was. "No," she added in case he needed further clarification.

"Why not?" His challenge was almost like idle curiosity. Pithy and confident he'd eventually get his way.

She goggled at him. "That train wreck last night for starters," she blurted, face seared with a mask of humiliated embarrassment. If he'd made a pass and she'd rejected him, that would be one thing, but the way she'd responded had been horribly revealing. She dropped her gaze, wishing she could take back her reaction, especially when it occurred to her he might use it to get what he wanted.

"So the chemistry between us is alive and well. We've successfully ignored it in the past. Maybe we'll even look at resuming that side of our relationship once you're fully recovered. It's got nothing to do with my desire to raise my daughter."

Sirena choked. "What relationship? What chemistry?" Incredulous, she leaped to her feet without being aware of it. Her entire being rejected everything he was saying. It was so cruel she couldn't bear it. "I'm moving back to my flat as soon as the doctor clears me." She threw her napkin on the table and started to walk out again.

"You're going alone," he said in an implacable tone that chilled her to her marrow. "Lucy is staying here."

Slam. Here it was. The brick wall she had always known he would push between her and her child. Had she actually felt herself softening toward him? He was a bastard, through and through. And it hurt! He was hurting her by treating her this way and he was hurting her by not being the man she wanted him to be.

"That is not what our *legally binding* agreement says," she whirled to state.

"Keep your lawyer on retainer, sweetheart. We're going to rewrite it."

He wasn't bluffing. Her heart twisted while the rest of her, the part that had lost to a bully once before, put up her dukes. She had never wanted to physically harm anyone in her life, but at this moment a swelling wave of injustice pushed her toward him in aggressive confrontation, muscles twitching with the desire to claw him apart because he was striking at her very foundation.

He rose swiftly as she approached, surprised and instantly guarded, taking on a ready stance, his size the only thing that stopped her from lashing out with everything in her.

"Well, isn't that like you," she said with the only weapon available: a tongue coated with enough resentful hatred it wielded itself. *"I want you, Sirena,"* she mocked. *"Touch me, Sirena.* And the next morning it's, take everything that matters to her and kick her to the curb. Go ahead. Send me into John's office for another pile of legal bills I can't afford. I'll raise the stakes and take this to the court of public opinion. I'll hurt you in every way I can find. I'll take your daughter, because I will *not* let her be raised by someone who treats people the way you do."

She wiped the back of her wrist across her lips, her incensed emotions deflating to despair as she heard her own words and knew that she was bravado against his arsenal of money, position and power. What did she have? Charges against her for theft.

She couldn't continue to face him without breaking down.

"Where do you get the nerve to judge *me?*" she managed as a parting shot before she decamped to higher ground.

Raoul stood in astonished silence as he listened to Sirena's retreat. He felt as though he'd just surprised a wounded lioness and barely escaped still clutching his vital organs. Adrenaline stung his arteries and he had to consciously tell his muscles to relax.

None of that closed what felt like a giant chasm in his chest. *Touch me, Sirena. Kick her to the curb.* Shame snaked through him, keeping his jaw clenched even though he wanted to shout back at her in defense. *He* was the one with the right to trust issues. Where did she get off accusing *him* of manipulation?

His housekeeper came through, startling him. "More coffee?" she asked, obviously surprised to see the table deserted.

"No," he barked, then pulled himself together. "No, thank you," he said with more control, rubbing his face then disheveling his hair. "Please make up some sandwiches for Sirena, since she didn't finish her breakfast. I'll be in my office."

He went there for privacy, to work through their confrontation, not to make a dent in the work that piled up every minute he was distracted by this new family of his.

Just a daughter, he reminded himself. Not a partner.

Touch me. His gut tightened in remembered ecstasy as he felt again her light fingers encircling him. Desire had exploded in him last night. For her. Despite all his attempts to make excuses, the sad truth was no other woman tempted him. Even before conceiving Lucy, he'd been taking women to dinner without taking anything else.

He didn't want Sirena to be the only one he wanted. He ought to have more control over himself. As he'd eschewed sleep this morning in favor of forming arguments to keep Sirena and Lucy living with him, he'd convinced himself it was a convenient solution to their custody battle, nothing to do with sexual attraction.

While he'd relived her soft mewling noises and passionate response to his kiss in the hallway, her body incapable of lying.

Sirena didn't want anything to do with him, though. Maybe she was physically attracted, but her ferocity this morning warned him that she would rather smother him in his sleep than share his bed for lovemaking.

He stared blindly at the colorful gardens beyond his office window, his mind's eye seeing her savaged expression the day at the gate, then again this morning. A hard hand closed around his heart, squeezing uncomfortably. A million times he'd told himself she was as jaded and detached as all the rest of his lovers, but today something admonished him. He feared he'd hurt her in a way he hadn't realized he could. But how was his treatment of her any different than hers of him? She had gotten him depending on her, then backhanded him with theft. She'd ruined him for other women and was completely wrong for him at the same time.

Movement caught his eye. Sirena had brought Lucy into the garden. She wore a summer dress and bare feet. Her hair hung in a damp curtain down her back, its curls weighted into subtle waves that would spring up as the sun dried it. Folding one leg under herself the way she often did, she sat on the covered swing and kicked it into a gentle rock, head tilting back as she inhaled deeply.

She was pure woman in that moment, sensual yet maternal. Beautiful.

The want in him took on a new, disconcerting depth. It wasn't just sexual. He remembered her efficiency, her smooth handling of difficult people, her quick smiles.

He wanted the Sirena he'd believed her to be before his dented bank balance had proved she wasn't.

Damn it, he didn't *do* complex relationships. Mother-son. Simple. Protective big brother. Easy. Boss and employee. Black-and-white.

With one noted exception.

His father's suicide over what had seemed to be a sordid yet standard affair was earning some of his empathy. If his father had struggled with things like overstepping boundaries in the workplace and a lust that battled strength with his love for his child, Raoul could see where he'd felt torn in too many directions. Raoul wasn't anywhere near killing himself over it, but he wasn't getting much sleep.

But if he was about to be exposed for his perfidy, he might start thinking drastic thoughts. Sirena had threatened a publicity backlash and he believed her. He was learning there was a no-holds-barred quality when her basic rights were threatened and part of him respected her for it.

And if there was one thing he prided himself on, it was upholding his end of a bargain.

Cursing, he opened the French doors onto the patio and strolled across to Sirena, footsteps whispering across the grass. Her eyes opened, but only to slits.

"I'm floating down the river of denial. Don't kill the mood," she warned with a chilly edge to her soft tone.

The corner of his mouth quirked. She had always caught him off guard with her colorful expressions. There was a hidden poet in her, he suspected. A romantic.

He frowned, unable to fit that with the calculating vamp he knew her to be.

"Look," he said, sweeping her multiple facets aside to work at keeping things simple. He'd been angry when he'd thrown his ultimatum at her, grumpily aware that he wanted her rather desperately while she thought he was trying to manipulate her. The manipulating factor was this infernal chemistry!

"I was wrong to say I'd go back on our agreement. You're right. You negotiated in good faith and things between us will only get ugly if we don't talk these things through without using Lucy as leverage."

"Are you on drugs? I thought you said I was right." Her eyes stayed shut, not revealing any of the willingness to compromise he was looking for.

"Where is all this sass coming from?" he demanded. "You never used to say things like that to me."

"Sure I did. In my head. Now that you've fired me, I can use my outside voice."

He accepted that with a disgruntled press of his lips, pushing his hands into his pockets as he rocked on his heels. The sun on his back was so hot he could feel the burn through his shirt. Sirena and the baby were in the shade, though, so he didn't insist they go back into the house yet.

"Will you stay? You know what my workload is like. I have to travel and I don't want to be half a globe from Lucy, not for weeks at a time."

"So when you say stay, you mean follow you around like nomads?" Her eyes opened, lashes screening her thoughts, but the indignant lift of her brows said plenty.

"Why not? You liked the travel when you worked for me, didn't you?"

Sirena pursed her lips. "When I got out of the hotels to see the sights."

He frowned, sensing criticism when he was well aware

she'd enjoyed visiting foreign cultures, welcoming new people and perspectives with excited curiosity, always ready with small talk full of well-researched questions about museums or local wonders, always craning her head at markets when they passed. She made good use of all she learned too, providing tidbits that informed his negotiations through foreign bureaucracy, but he wondered suddenly if he'd kept her too busy to actually experience all she'd wanted to.

They'd been there to work, though. That's what he did and who he was.

He scowled as he contemplated how little of those countries *he'd* seen.

"It doesn't matter what I want," she sighed. "Lucy will have school—"

"Years down the road," he argued, not letting her finish. "I'll make allowances for that, but you know as well as I do it will take time to put things in place. For the next few years, as long as she has us, she'll be happy anywhere. I'm not talking about leaving tomorrow. I realize you have medical checkups. We'll stay here as long as you need, but later in the year I don't see why we can't take a few weeks in Milan. My mother is already asking when I'll bring her to New York."

"I can't live with you permanently. How would we explain it to people? Your future bedmates sure wouldn't like it, and what if one of us wants to get married?"

Irritated by the mention of bedmates and life mates, he dismissed both. "I've never been interested in marriage and see even less point now. As for bedmates, for Lucy's sake, we should keep that in-house."

Sirena suddenly stopped the swing. Raoul sensed refusal so tangibly he bristled.

"Wow. For Lucy's sake I ought to have sex with you?

That's the kind of reasoning even someone with my dam-aged morals has trouble following."

"If we sleep together, it'll be because we both want to," he snapped, aware he was handling this badly, but she was frustrating the hell out of him. "That train wreck last night was a head-on crash from both sides. You want me and when you get cleared by the doctor, you'll be cleared for sex. Think about *that*."

CHAPTER SIX

SIRENA DIDN'T HAVE much choice about whether to think on it. Her body was enamored with the idea of falling into bed with her old boss. Her mind drifted in that direction at the least bit of encouragement. Asleep, awake… He was always nearby, smelling like manly aftershave or endearingly like baby powder, telling family secrets to Lucy or speaking in some sexy foreign language on the phone, the syllables drifting teasingly into her ears…

She got so she conjured reasons not to trust him in order to counter the attraction, which wasn't healthy. *I've never been interested in marriage and see even less point now.* That certainly told her where his interest in her as a *bedmate* started and stopped.

They wound up having abbreviated conversations punctuated by glances of awareness and stubborn avoidances. She *had* to move back into her own flat.

The trouble was, her neighbor's niece was still begging to take it over. Sirena began thinking that if she could find a decent job in a less-expensive part of London, she might be able to keep renting out her existing flat and take something smaller for herself. Her flat was an asset she didn't want to lose and without a better income soon, she would. Even at that, she wasn't sure how she'd pay for day care so she could work.

Which was the sort of worn path of worry that made her

circle back to what Raoul was offering. But it would be so *wrong.* He had wronged her and continued to feel wronged *by* her. She might have drunk herself into oblivion out of frustration if she didn't have a baby to think of. At least she could meet a friend for a small one.

Raoul didn't know what to make of her announcement that she was going out for the evening. His brows almost went through his hairline, but she didn't let that deter her.

"Amber is a friend who moved to Canada years ago. She's coming into London tonight. It's her only free time, so I'd like to join her for tapas and a drink and leave Lucy with you."

"Are you sure you're up for it?" he asked with one of those sweeping glances that lit fires all over her.

"Of course," she said more stridently than she intended, but the way she tingled every time he so much as turned his head in her direction was driving her crazy. She couldn't wait to get Amber's objective view of this situation.

With a shrug, Raoul said, "Pack a bag and we'll stay at the penthouse. That way you won't be so late getting in and I can go into the office in the morning. We'll test-drive one aspect of this arrangement I've suggested."

One aspect. Part of her wanted to refuse on principle, but she liked the idea of a shorter trip home. Her doctor was pleased with her progress, but between Lucy's needs and her body's wants, she wasn't sleeping enough.

And by the time she'd packed, driven in, unpacked and settled the baby, she was ready for bed, not a night on the town. She put on a black skirt and ruffled green top anyway. Both were a bit tight. At least her hair was an asset. She'd been clipping it up for months and hadn't realized how much it had grown. She rather liked it clouding around her shoulders, drawing attention from her still-thick waist. Wearing heels and makeup for the first time in ages, she looked pretty good.

Echoes of her stepmother's critical voice swept through her, cataloging her flaws and bringing Sirena down a smidge, but she had been practicing how to block that painful denigration for years. She stood straight and ignored the whispers of insecurity, jumping when Raoul appeared in her bedroom doorway.

"*Who* is this Amber?" he asked in a dark growl.

"A friend from school." Sirena turned from the mirror, a wicked slide of excitement careening through her as she took him in.

He wore jeans and a button-down shirt open at his throat, cuffs rolled up to his forearms. He was the man who always made butterflies invade her middle.

"You dress like this for a woman?" His gaze made a slow, thorough study of her from collarbone to ankles.

"This is all that fits. I can't show up in my sweats and trainers. Or do you mean I look like a pile of socks pushed into a leg of tights? Should I change?" Her hand went to the zip of her skirt.

His expression was dumbfounded. "Yes. *No,*" he insisted. "You look fine. Excellent. Beautiful. You're not meeting a man?"

"Because my dating profile of 'unemployed new mum with custody issues' is so irresistible? No. I'm meeting a *girl*friend. I wish you would quit calling me a liar."

"I called you beautiful," he said with a raking glance of masculine hunger, his frown both askance and…not critical, but not pleased.

She curled her toes in her shoes, disconcerted by how admiring and possessive he seemed. "I wasn't fishing for flattery."

He barred the door with his arm.

An uncomfortable silence stretched as her stepmother's voice did a number on her again, cataloging the extra pounds and shadows under her eyes and lack of a manicure, but as Raoul skimmed his gaze down her figure once more, and his expression reflected nothing but male approval, she felt quite beautiful.

The swirling sensation in her abdomen redoubled and little sensors in her body began reaching out toward him, tugging her with magnetic power toward him.

She forced herself to stand still, but he dropped his arm and stepped forward until he was standing right in front of her, towering despite her heels. His gray eyes shone with a startlingly warm regard as he scanned her face and hair. Strong hands came up to frame her face with disconcerting tenderness.

Her breath stalled in her lungs as he started to bend his head, his gaze on her mouth.

"What are you doing?" she managed, pressing against his chest.

He paused, gaze smoky with intent. "Reminding you that if a man comes on to you tonight, you have one right here willing to satisfy your needs."

He began to lower his head again but she leaned away.

"Don't smudge my lipstick," she argued shakily, the best protest she could rouse when her whole body wanted to let his take over. Her breasts ached for contact with the hardness of his chest and heat pooled between her thighs. A fine trembling invaded her limbs, making her weak. Her arms longed to reach out and cling to him.

At the last second, he veered to bury his lips against her neck. His light stubble abraded her skin while his open mouth found a sensitive spot on her nape that took out her knees.

"What are you doing?" she cried, melting into the arms that caught her. Her nipples sharpened into hard points as he applied delicate suction, marking her.

She should have stopped him, but she was held not just by his strength, but by a paralysis of physical joy. Her mouth ached for the press of his while her mind became a turmoil of unconscious thoughts, processing only the sensations of knowing hands skimming her curves as he laid claim to her hips and bottom. He was hard, ready, so tempting—

"You make me lose my mind," he growled, steadying her before he released her. "Do not start anything with anyone tonight. The car is waiting. That's what I came to tell you." He walked out.

Raoul didn't resent Sirena taking a night out, but he didn't like having no right to question her comings and goings and suspected the reason was old-fashioned jealousy. *Not* an emotion he'd ever experienced, and definitely unwelcome, but she was so hot. As sexy as a year ago, but less buttoned-down and professional. With her hair loose and her full breasts brimming her top, he'd seen what every man in London would see: a beautiful woman.

And he wouldn't be there to warn them off with a don't-even-try-it stare.

He shouldn't have kissed her, but he hadn't been able to resist imprinting her with the knowledge he wanted her. She'd been skittishly avoiding him since their kiss outside Lucy's bedroom and he'd been trying to ignore how badly he craved her, but his hunger grew exponentially every day.

It was frustrating as hell, but no matter how uncomfortable they both were with each other, they were equally devoted to Lucy. He couldn't countenance anything more than a few hours of separation from his child, so he kept coming back to sharing his house with her mother.

Disgruntled, still smelling of her perfume, he waited in the foyer to watch her leave, arms folded.

Sirena appeared, checked her step and flushed. Ducking her head, she opened her pocketbook. "I have my phone if Lucy needs me."

"We'll be fine. Do you have David's number?" he asked, mentioning his London driver.

"Yes, it's programmed—" She swept her thumb across the screen and frowned. "Oh, I missed this from Amber. She's sick. That's disappointing."

More like devastating, if her body language was anything to go by. Raoul was disgustingly relieved, but as he watched her shoulders fall and the pretty glow of excitement extinguish from her expression, he couldn't help feeling sorry for her.

She tempered her sad pout into a resigned quirk. "All dressed up and no place to go," she said wryly. "Sorry to drag you all the way to London for nothing. I guess it'll be sweats and trainers after all. I'll just let her know I got the message…" She ducked her head to text a reply.

"You were really looking forward to this," he commented as she finished.

She shrugged. "We chat online, but it's like with my sister. Sometimes I want to see her and it's frustrating when I can't." She blinked and he thought he glimpsed tears, but she started back to her room.

"Sirena."

She stiffened, not turning. "Yes?"

He'd surely regret this, but there was something about the brave face she was putting on and hell, she looked amazing. He couldn't let this butterfly crawl back into her shapeless cocoon.

"Come have a drink with me." He jerked his head toward the unlit lounge.

"What? No. Why? I'll be feeding Lucy later. I can't."

How many shades of refusal was that, he wondered with a twinge between amusement and exasperation.

"We'll stick to the plan," he countered. "Have the glass of wine you were planning to have with your friend and

I'll feed Lucy a bottle when she needs it. Going out was obviously something you were anticipating."

"It wasn't the wine." She rolled her eyes. "I wanted to see my friend."

"So come tell me why she's so special to you." He herded her toward the lounge and suspected she only let him because she was trying to pull away from contact with his palm against the small of her back.

"I don't understand why you'd want me to." She scuffed her spiky heels as he crowded her into the room with the sunken conversation area and the wet bar in the corner. He gave up trying to steer her and walked ahead of her, turning on a lamp on the end table before he brought the track lighting over the bar up to half power, keeping the mood soothing and intimate.

"You keep accusing me of not taking time to ask about your life. And…" He gestured at where her leg peeked from the slit in her skirt to the ruffles that framed her cleavage. "I can't stand the idea of this going to waste. I'd take you out, but unlike you I haven't arranged a sitter. Here. Have a seat and tell the bartender about your day."

He held one of the high stools and she hesitated before warily scooting her hip onto it. He let his gaze linger on the curve of her pert backside as it flowed into the slope of her lower back. Damn, but he wanted to stroke and claim.

Thief, he reminded himself, but it didn't do much to quell his hunger. Rounding the bar, he looked for a suitably light white wine in the small cooler.

"I should tell David he's off for the night," she said in a tone that put him back a year. Efficient, forward with responsibility and attention to detail, lilting just enough to invite a correction if she was off course. She rarely ever had been, except—

As she placed the call, he gestured for the phone.

She handed it across, brows lifted with inquiry.

He enlightened her as he made his request of David. "We've had a change of plans. Can you run to Angelo's and ask them to make us a couple of plates? Whatever they have on special, but no mushrooms for Sirena. You can go home after that."

"Are we working late?" she mused facetiously.

"I don't feel like cooking. Do you?"

"*Can* you cook? I've never seen you try."

"I can grill a steak." He was currently polishing glasses like a pro, having picked up both skills working in restaurants for much-needed cash a long time ago.

"But a man in your position never *has* to do anything, does he?" Her lips curved in a deprecating smile, niggling him into a serious response.

"I'm always irritated by the suggestion I haven't worked for what I have. I might have been born into a life of privilege, but that bottomed out thanks to my stepfather. Everything I have I built myself, and it comes with obligations and responsibilities that take up time. If I can delegate the small things, like cooking a steak, so I can negotiate a union contract to keep myself and a few hundred people working and fed, I will." He poured two glasses and pushed one toward her.

She looked at her wine, then gave him a glance of re-assessment. Lifting her glass, she awaited the soft clink of his.

"To pleasant conversations between old friends," she said with gentle mockery.

He leaned back on the far side of the space behind the bar, eyeing her through slitted lids. "I can't get used to this."

"Used to what?" She set down her glass and rotated her knees forward so she faced him, elbows braced on the bar's marble top.

"This woman full of backchat and sarcasm. The one with secrets and a double life. The real you."

She might have flinched, but her chin quickly came forward to a defiant angle. Her gaze stayed low, showing him a rainbow of subtle shadows on her eyelids. "You're attributing me with more mystery than I possess. Yes, I'm being more frank with you than I was, but you can't tell your boss he's being an arrogant jerk, can you?" She lifted her lashes to level a hard stare at him. "Not if you want to pay the bills."

He thought about letting this devolve into something serious, but opted to keep things friendly. "I wouldn't have fired you for saying that," he assured her, waiting a beat before adding, "I would have said you were wrong."

Her mouth twitched, then she let the laugh happen and he experienced a sensation like settling into your own sofa or bed. *Definitely a bed,* he thought as a tingle of pure, masculine craving rose inside him. He let himself admire her painted lips and graceful throat and the exposed alabaster skin on her chest to the swells of her breasts. Why had he never taken her to dinner before?

Oh, right. She had been working for him.

It was freeing not to have that obstacle between them anymore.

Slow down, he reminded himself as she sobered and flicked a glance in his direction. The sexual undercurrents might be acknowledged, finally, but just because he wanted to bed her didn't mean he should.

Sirena couldn't take the intense way Raoul was staring at her. Every single day of working for him, she'd longed for him to show some sign of interest in her. Now that he had, it scared the hell out of her. But then, she knew better than to trust he was genuinely interested.

Accosted by harsh memories, she slid off the bar stool and took her wine to the expansive glass windows where the London Eye and the rest of the waterfront stained the river with neon rainbows.

"So is this how you start all your flashy dates? Or do they end here?"

"Flashy?" His image, only partially visible in the dim reflection on the glass, came around the bar to stand like a specter behind her.

"Women line up for the privilege, so I assume a date with you is pretty fantastic. Are they impressed when you bring them back here for a nightcap?" And a thorough see-ing to? *Don't think about it.*

"I don't go out of my way to impress, if that's what you're implying. Dinner. A show. Does that differ hugely from one of your dates?"

She cut him a pithy look over her shoulder. "Since when do I have time to date?"

He absorbed that with a swallow of wine. "You've sug-gested a few times that I overworked you, but you also want me to believe your private life included a man who could have fathered Lucy. Which is the truth?"

"I was saving face when I said that," she admitted to the window.

"So I was an ogre who demanded too much? You could have said something."

Sirena hitched a shoulder, bothered that she felt guilty for not standing up for herself. "I didn't want to let you down or make you think I couldn't handle it." There was her stepmother walking into the room again, tsking with dissatisfaction, setting the bar another notch higher so Si-rena would never, ever reach it, no matter how hard she tried. But oh, how she tried, hating to fail and draw criti-cism. "Some of that's my own baggage. I'm a workaholic. You can relate, I'm sure."

He moved to stand beside her. "I thought you were

happy with the workload. It didn't occur to me I was kill-ing your social life. You must have felt a lot of resentment."

He was jumping to the conclusion that that's why she'd stolen from him.

"No." Annoyed, she walked to the far end of the win-dows. "I never had a social life, so there was nothing to kill."

"You weren't a virgin. There was at least one man in your life," he shot back.

"One," she agreed, staring into the stemmed glass. "His name was Stephan. We lived together for almost two years, but we were both starving students, so date night was mi-crowave popcorn and whatever movie was on the telly." Stephan had had about a thousand allergies, including al-cohol, so even a cheap wine or beer had been out of the question. "Sometimes we went crazy and rented a new release, but my hand-me-down player said 'bad disc' half the time, so it wasn't worth the hassle."

"You *lived* with him?" Raoul's brows went up in askance reaction.

"It's not the same as dating," she hurried to argue. "It was—" Convenient. A desperate act in a lonely time. A mistake.

"Serious?" he supplied in a honed voice. He moved a few steps closer, seeming confrontational, which discon-certed her.

"Why are you judging me?" She rounded the conver-sation area, circling back to the bar, where she took a big gulp of wine before she set down her glass. "All I'm say-ing is that I never dated. This is turning into a long con-versation about nothing."

"You lived with a man for two years. That's not noth-ing, Sirena. Did you talk about marriage?"

"I—" She didn't want to go there, still feeling awful about it. Crossing her arms, she admitted, "He proposed.

It didn't work out." There, that was vague enough to keep her from looking as bad as she felt.

"You were *engaged*—"

"Shh! You're going to wake Lucy," she hissed. "Why are you yelling? I'm sorry I said anything." She looked for her watch, but she'd removed it because it didn't go with this outfit. "David should be here with the meals soon, shouldn't he?"

Raoul could barely compute what he was hearing. Another man had been that close to locking Sirena into marriage forever. How could he not have known?

"Did working for me cause the breakup?" he asked with a swift need to know.

"No." She sounded annoyed.

"What then?" For some reason this was important. He needed to know she'd severed all ties with this other man, irrevocably. "Do you still have feelings for him?"

"I'll always love him," she said with a self-conscious shrug.

The words rocked him onto his heels, like the back draft from a semitruck that nearly flattened him.

"In a friend way. That's all it ever was. A friend thing. Do you really need all the gory details?"

"I do, yes," he said through lips that felt stiff and cold. He wondered how he'd kept his wine from spilling, because he'd forgotten he held the glass. He moved to set it on an end table before giving Sirena his full attention, still reeling with shock when really, it wasn't as if people living together was a scandal. He just hadn't realized she had been so deeply involved with anyone. Ever.

When he lifted his gaze to prompt her into continuing, a shadow of persecution clouded her expression.

"It was a lonely time in my life. Amber was in Canada, my family had left for Australia. Stephan was the first boy who'd ever noticed me—"

"I find that hard to believe," Raoul interjected.

"The first boy I'd ever noticed had noticed me, then. Maybe there were crushes before that, but I wasn't allowed to go out when I was living at home—not even to spend the night at Amber's, in case we snuck out to a party. My stepmother wasn't having a pregnant teenager on her watch, so there were chores and a curfew and a little sister to babysit. When I enrolled at college, Stephan was the first boy I had the opportunity to spend time with. He was nice and I was romantic enough to spin it into more than it was." She shrugged again, looking as though she wanted to end there.

"It was obviously more if he proposed."

"That was impulse on his part. I decided to quit my degree and go with the business certificate so I could start earning proper money, rather than temping and doing transcription around my courses. He was afraid I'd meet someone else and I realized I wanted to, so we broke up."

Raoul felt a shred of pity for the man's desperate measure that hadn't paid off. At the same time, he was relieved, which unsettled him. He saw nothing but misery and remorse in her, though. "A puppy love relationship isn't anything to be ashamed of. Why do you feel guilty?" he asked.

"Because I hurt him. Part of me wonders if I wasn't using him because I was broke and didn't have anywhere else to turn. I didn't mean to lead him on, but I did."

The buzzer announced David with their meals.

Raoul turned to let him up, but all he could think was, *You used me. Do you feel bad about that?*

CHAPTER SEVEN

TYPICAL OF ANGELO'S welcoming charm as a restaurateur, he had sent along a single white rose with a silk ribbon tied to the stem. *We've missed you,* the tag read.

Sirena stifled a pang of wistfulness as she picked up the budding flower from where it sat next to her plate and searched for a hint of scent in the tightly closed petals.

David had brought the basket of chinaware and scrumptious smells to the table beside the pool, setting it out in a way she imagined he'd done for countless of Raoul's paramours. Everything glittered, from the silver to the candles flames to the stars and city lights winking in the warm night air. Raoul set relaxing acoustic guitar music to come through the outdoor speakers and arrived with their glasses.

His brows went up with silent inquiry.

"Fast asleep," Sirena answered. She had known Lucy would be, but checking on her had been a timely excuse to leave Raoul's intense presence. She wasn't sure she was ready to face him again.

A distant beep sounded, signaling that David had left the apartment. They were alone again. *Round two,* she thought and reached for the wine Raoul set above her knife tip. He had topped up her glass, bringing the temperature of the pinot grigio down a degree so it soothed her throat as she drank.

She hesitated to start eating, even though the food was Angelo's typical appetizing fare of creamy pasta, bright peppers and fragrant basil. This wasn't like all those other times when she and Raoul had a tablet or laptop between them and she had chewed between typing and answering calls. They'd never stood on ceremony while working, but this was anything but casual. More than ever, she was aware of Raoul's potent masculinity, his quiet habits of sharp observation, his undeniable air of command.

And she was hyperaware of her dolled-up attire, the way even Angelo seemed to know this was different and had added the extra touch of silver and china.

This felt like a date.

"Problem?" Raoul asked.

She shook her head, chastising herself for falling into old fantasies of romance. "Just thinking I should put this in water," she said, gesturing to the rose.

"It can wait until we've eaten," he said.

He seemed to be waiting for her to start and that made her nervous. She searched for a neutral topic to break what felt like a tense silence. He spoke first.

"Why didn't you go to Australia with your family?"

Oh, hell, they were going there, were they? It wasn't enough to pry open the oyster, making her feel as though her protective shell was snapped in half and left with jagged edges. No, he wanted to poke a finger into her vulnerable center and see if there was a pearl in there, one glossed over for years, but gritty as obsidian at its heart.

She licked sauce from the corner of her mouth, stating plainly, "I wasn't invited."

He lowered his fork as his brilliant mind absorbed what was a logical and sensible answer, yet didn't make sense at all. He frowned. "Why weren't you invited?"

She held back a rude snort at a question she'd never been able to answer. Picking up the napkin off her lap, she dried her lips, wondering if she'd be able to get through this plate of food when her appetite was fading so quickly.

"I had just started school," she said, offering the excuse Faye, her stepmother, had used. "My father had given me some money toward tuition, about the same amount as airfare. It didn't make sense to throw it away."

"So you were given a choice between school and going with them?"

"No." She couldn't help the bluster of resentment that hardened the word. Old, angry tension started clenching up her insides and she had to make a conscious effort not to let it take her over. Picking up her fork, she deflected the subject a little.

"This is why I was looking forward to dinner with Amber. She knows my history with my stepmother and lets me vent about whatever is bothering me, without my having to lay the groundwork and examine how much is my fault and whether I'm being paranoid. Amber takes my side, which is refreshing, whereas if I try to explain it all to you—" she waved a hand toward him, feeling herself getting worked up, but unable to stop it "—you'll be like Stephan and say maybe Faye didn't mean it that way, that I'm being oversensitive and her reasons make sense and I'm misinterpreting. Her reasons *always* make sense, Raoul. That's the beauty of her dictatorship."

Oh, God, shut up, Sirena.

She clenched her teeth, intending to drop the subject, but she couldn't hide the way her hand trembled as she tried to twirl noodles onto the tines of her fork.

"Why don't you give me an example," he suggested in a tone that echoed with reasonability, as though he were trying to talk a crazy person off a window ledge.

Sirena crammed too big a bite into her mouth, but he waited her out, saying nothing as she chewed and swallowed. The pasta went down like a lump of coal, acrid and coarse.

"For instance," she said tightly, "when I was so pregnant and swollen I could hardly get myself out of bed, worried I would *die,* I asked if my sister could come and was told that my father's plumbing business had fallen off and Ali had exams and the doctors were keeping an eye on Faye's thyroid so the timing really didn't work."

She glanced up to see a frozen expression on his face. "You should have called *me.*"

A pang of anguish struck. She'd been tempted a million times, but replied, "The people who were supposed to love and care about me wouldn't come. What was the point in asking you?"

He jerked back as if she'd thrown her pasta in his face.

She looked away, trying to hide the fact she was growing teary over old conflicts that would never be resolved. Her stepmother cared nothing for her while she, Sirena, loved her father and sister. There was nothing that could be done except manage the situation.

After a few seconds, he inquired in a stiff tone, "What about Amber? Why didn't you call her, if you're such good friends?"

"She's in a wheelchair." She cleared the huskiness from her throat. "Which isn't to say she wouldn't have been a help, but my flat is a walk-up and she has other health problems. That's what brought her to London. She's seeing a specialist then heading straight home."

His silence rang with pointed surprise. "I really don't know anything about you."

She wasn't touching that with a ten-foot pole.

They ate in silence for a few minutes until he asked, "Your father wasn't worried about you?"

"Of course, but he remarried because he didn't know

what to do with a little girl. He wasn't about to play mid-wife to a grown woman."

"And your sister? She can't make her own decisions?"

Sirena let out a poignant sigh, bristling at his judgment because if he didn't understand Ali's vulnerability and how much she needed support, he'd never understand why she'd taken his money for the young woman.

"Ali's young for her age. She struggles in school, so exams are a real issue for her. Pitting her against her mother has never seemed right, no matter how much I've wanted to. I adore her like I can't even tell you and I miss her terribly. I practically raised her. Faye wouldn't change a nappy if I was around to do it. Homework was me, running flash cards and spelling lists. The questions about puberty and sex and buying her first bra all came to me. But they left nearly eight years ago and I haven't seen her since. Faye had been cooking up the move the whole time I was applying to school, never mentioning it until my plans were sealed. Tell me that's not small-minded and hurtful."

"You could have gone to see them."

"Oh, with all my spare time working two jobs while studying? Or do you mean after you hired me? Go all the way to Australia for one of those generous single weeks you'd allow me? Every time I asked for more than five days you'd get an expression on your face like you were passing a kidney stone. I tried taking a stretch after that trade fair in Tokyo, but the database melted down in Brussels, remember? I had to cancel."

A muscle ticked in his cheek. "You might have explained the circumstances."

"To what end, Raoul? You never once showed the least bit of interest in my private life. You wanted an extension of your laptop, not a living, breathing woman."

"Because you were my employee," he bit out, pushing away from the table in a minor explosion.

She'd seen him reach the limit of his patience, but usually within the context of a business deal going south. To have that aggressive male energy aimed at her made her sit very still, but he wasn't throwing his anger at her. He paced to the edge of the pool, where he shoved his hands into his pockets and scowled into the eerie glow of the blue-green depths.

"You have no idea what it's like to lust after your co-worker, knowing that's the one person off-limits."

I beg to differ, she thought, but swallowed it back because… She shook her head. "How can you say something like that when you made it quite clear—"

"I know what I said that day. Stop throwing it in my face," he growled. "Why do you think I let it go so far so fast in Oxshott? I'd been thinking about it for two solid years. And the next day—" he gestured in frustration "—the very next day, I found you'd been stealing. You betrayed my trust and you used me. What the hell was I supposed to say? Admit you'd hurt me? It was too humiliating."

She'd *hurt* him?

No. She didn't let herself believe it, not after all these months of scouring the joy and tenderness from her memories, reframing it as a meaningless one-afternoon stand. Maybe in her mind their day in Oxshott had been special, but all he was saying was that he'd had sexual feelings for her while she'd been employed by him. That was only a fraction more personal than being *handy.* His ego had been damaged, not his heart.

"I was trying to behave like a professional as well," she said thinly. "Not dragging my personal life into the office. I don't see the point in sharing it now." She plucked her napkin from her lap and dropped it beside her plate. "You still don't care and I still can't see my family."

"What makes you think I don't care?" he swung around to challenge.

His naked look of strong emotion was a spear straight into her heart. She averted her gaze, tempted to dissect what sort of feelings underpinned his intense question, but refusing to. That way lay madness.

"Don't," she said through a tight throat. "You hate me and I'm fine with that because I hate you, too." *Liar*, a voice whispered in her head, but she ignored it along with the hiss of his sharp inhale. "Let's just keep things as honest as possible. For Lucy's sake."

It was hard to look at him, but she made herself do it. Made herself look him in the eye and face his hatred with stillness and calm while she wrapped tight inner arms around her writhing soul.

"I wish it was that simple." He surged forward to grip the back of his chair. "I want to hate you, but now I understand why you felt you couldn't come to me. You didn't know I was acting uninterested to curb my attraction, but it was there all along."

She recoiled, swinging from disbelief to heart-pounding excitement to intense hurt that he had treated her the way he had regardless of having feelings for her. They weren't very strong if he could behave like that, were they?

Speaking very carefully, crushing her icy fingers together in her lap, she stated the obvious. "Lust is not caring, Raoul."

He straightened to an arrogant height.

"No, listen," she rushed on, fearing he thought she was begging for affection. "I didn't think one hookup meant we were getting married and living happily ever after. I'm just saying I thought you had some respect and regard for me. But even a dismissal slip would have been better than having me arrested without speaking to me. That was…"

She faltered. He was staring at her with an expression

that had gone stony. Steeling herself, she forced herself to continue, even though her voice thinned.

"Discovering I was pregnant, knowing they'd take the baby from me in prison—" She stood in a shaken need to retreat, very afraid she was going to start to cry as the memories closed in. "Even my stepmother didn't go that far to hurt me."

"I didn't know you were pregnant," he reminded her ferociously.

"Exactly! And if you did, you would have gone easy for the baby's sake, not mine. You didn't care about *me*. Not one bit."

CHAPTER EIGHT

RAOUL FELT AS though he was pacing in London's infamous fog. The walls of his penthouse were clear enough, the sky beyond the windows dull with a high ceiling, but his mind wouldn't grasp a lucid concept. He kept replaying everything Sirena had said last night, which had him writhing in a miasma of regret and agitation.

Lucy squirmed in his hold.

He paused to look at her, certain she must be picking up his tension. That's why she was so unsettled. He was pacing one end of his home to the other trying to soothe her, but neither of them was finding any peace.

How peaceful would Sirena have felt pacing a twelve-by-twelve cell?

His stomach churned.

He hadn't let himself dwell on that picture when he'd been trying to put her away, but now he couldn't get it out of his head. Vibrant Sirena who craned her neck with excited curiosity from the airport to the business center in every city they visited, locked in a cage of gray brick and cold bars.

You hate me and I'm fine with that because I hate you, too.

"What are you doing in here?"

Her voice startled him, causing a ripple of pleasure-pain down his spine. He blinked, becoming aware he'd wan-dered into the small flat off the main one. It was meant for a housekeeper or nanny, but stood empty because his maid service came daily to his city residence.

"Just something different for her to look at." He stopped rubbing Lucy's back and changed her position so she could see her mother. "She's fussy."

Sirena's brow crinkled as she took in the rumpled clothes he'd been wearing since their unfinished dinner by the pool.

His neutral expression felt too heavy on his cheekbones, but he balked at letting her see the more complex emotions writhing in him—uncertainty and yearning that went beyond the simply sexual. Pain. There was a searing throb inside him he couldn't seem to identify or ease.

"Have you been up all night? You should have brought her to me." She came forward to take the baby and was greeted with rooting kisses all over her face. She laughed with tender surprise, a sound that his angry attempt to jail her would have silenced forever. His heart shriveled in his chest.

"Did Daddy forget to feed you?" she murmured as she moved to the sofa.

"I tried a few minutes ago. She wasn't interested." His voice rasped.

She flinched at his rough tone, and flicked him an uncertain glance. "Giving him a hard time, are you?" She shrugged out of one side of her robe and dropped the strap of her tank top down her arm to expose her breast.

He had walked in on her feeding so many times she was no longer self-conscious about it. He didn't think of it as sexual, but seeing her feed their daughter affected him. It was the softness that overcame Sirena. Her fingers gently swirled Lucy's dark hair into whorls as the baby relaxed and made greedy noises. Her expression brimmed with such maternal love his breastbone ached.

He hadn't known she was pregnant when he'd pushed for jail time, but she had. She must have been terrified. While he, the first person she should have been able to rely on, had been the last person she would ever consider calling.

She glanced up. Her smile faded. Last night's enmity crept back like cold smoke, suffocating and dark. "I've got her," she said, dropping her lashes to hide her eyes. "You can get some sleep or go in to the office like you planned."

"No. I can't."

He ran a hand through his hair, becoming aware of a persistent headache and a general bruised feeling all over his body. His breath felt thick and insufficient. He spoke in a voice that very reluctantly delivered what he had to say.

"Sirena, you know I lost my father. What I never tell people...I found him. I came home from school and there he was, overdosed. Deliberately. He'd been having an affair with his secretary." He paused. "I called an ambulance, tried to revive him, but I was only nine years old. And it was too late."

Sirena's eyes fixated on him, the green orbs wide with shock. "I had no idea."

"I hate talking about it. My mother doesn't speak of it either."

"No, the few times she mentioned your father she sounded as if..."

"She loved him? She did. I only know about the affair because I found the note in the safe when we moved. It was full of assurances that he loved us both, but he still chose death because he couldn't live without this woman. I can't help blaming her." He knew it wasn't logical, but nothing about his father's death made sense to him.

"The note was the only thing left in the safe," he continued. "My stepfather had emptied it of everything else. My mother loved him, too, and he appeared to love her back.

I thought she'd found some comfort with him after our loss, but my stepfather was using her. He gambled away every cent we had. I came home from university because he'd had a heart attack and that's when I found the phones were about to be cut off and the electricity was overdue. We lost him and the house in the same month. My mother was a mess, grief stricken, but also feeling guilty for having trusted him and giving me no indication things were sliding downhill so fast."

He pushed his hands into his pockets, seeing again his mother's remorseful weeping and hearing her broken litany of, *He said he would turn it around.*

"You mentioned last night he was the reason you started over. I didn't realize it was that grim. What did you do?" Her voice was all softness and compassion, her bared shoulder enhancing the picture of her as vulnerable and incapable of causing harm.

"I developed a deep animosity toward anyone who tries to rob me," he admitted with quiet brutality.

She paled. Her gaze fell and her expression grew bleak.

"Maybe it doesn't excuse my having you arrested without speaking to you first, but I felt justified when it happened. I was… Damn it, Sirena, it was a perfect storm of my worst nightmares, falling for my secretary the way my father had, then being betrayed by someone I had come to rely on. I lashed out hard and fast."

She gave a little nod as she drew the sleepy infant off her breast and shrugged her robe into place. "I understand."

How many times had he seen that look on her face, he wondered, taking in the lowered lashes and stoic expression. He was tough to work for, he knew that. He pushed himself hard and was so overcommitted he didn't have time for mistakes. She'd always been the first to hear about any he found.

The phrase *long-suffering* came to mind as he saw past

her impassive expression to the self-protective tension in her body language. For the first time he heard the stark despondency in her voice. It had the same underlying incomprehension he felt when he talked about his father's suicide. She didn't understand. She was merely accepting what she couldn't change.

His heart lurched. He prided himself on supporting his family and living up to his responsibilities, but he had leaned heavily on Sirena when she worked for him. Where was her pillar of support, though? Her talk last night of being scared and ill and forsaken by her family had terrified and angered him anew. He wondered why she had needed the money. She had never said, but he was damned sure it wasn't for gambling debts or high fashion or drugs.

"Why did you steal from me, Sirena?"

She flinched at the word *steal,* then a kind of defeat washed over her, shutting her eyes and making her shoulders slump. "My sister needed money to pay her tuition fees."

The words left a bang of silence like a balloon popping into jagged pieces. He hadn't expected it, but it seemed oddly predictable after the fact.

She rushed on. "She was so upset after working so hard to get accepted to her degree program. They have a huge waiting list. She couldn't just wait a semester and apply again. And she'll make an amazing teacher, because she understands what it's like to struggle. I honestly thought it would only be for a few days until Dad got payment from his customer— Please don't go after him for repayment," she said with sudden stark alarm. "Things happened with his business. He doesn't have it and he's really struggling. It would kill him to know how much trouble I got myself into."

Her misery was real, her regret so palpable he could taste it. There was no struggle over whether to believe her.

The explanation fit perfectly with her revelations last night about her love for her sister. He'd always seen her as loyal. It was why he'd been so blindsided by and furious about her dishonesty. It was exactly like the woman he knew to step up and fix things as expediently as possible.

None of that excused her behavior, but at least he understood it.

"I think she'll go down for a while now." She rose, pale and not meeting his eyes.

He should have let her leave him to his thoughts, but put out his hand to stop her.

She halted, eyes downcast. Subtle waves of tension rolled off her. He could tell she wanted to be away from him, but she wasn't willing to allow contact with his outstretched arm even to brush it aside so she could leave the room.

Her refusal to touch him spread an ache of dismay through him. They'd torn the curtains back and exposed their motives for treating each other the way they had, but it didn't change the fact that she'd stolen and he'd wanted her jailed for it. Those sorts of injuries took a long time to heal.

But they had to ignore the pain and make this work in spite of it.

"The simplest, most advantageous solution for Lucy would be for us to live together permanently," he began.

Her shoulders sagged. "I know, Raoul. But it wouldn't work. We don't trust each other."

She seemed genuinely distressed. He felt the same, but he couldn't give up. It wasn't in his nature.

"We can start over. We've cleared the air. Damn it, Sirena," he rushed on when she shook her head. "I want to be with my daughter and you feel the same. You can't tell me you'd rather put her in day care for most of the time you'd have her. And when she's with me, I'm hiring a nanny to watch her so I can work? It makes no sense."

"But—"

"We put this behind us," he insisted, overriding her. "You just have to be honest from now on. Swear to me you'll never steal from me again. I want that promise," he stated firmly. More of an ultimatum, really.

Her eyes welled. He was coming at her from so many angles and she was still muddled from a rough sleep. She'd been deeply hurt last night. She'd tossed and turned, convinced that telling him anything about how badly he'd wounded her had been a mistake. What would he care? He would find a way to use it against her.

When she'd risen, she'd been determined to start the move back to her flat.

Then she'd found him looking like a pile of forgotten laundry, hair rumpled, sexy stubble on his cheeks and tortured shadows under his eyes. Her heart had been knocked out of place and was still sitting crooked in her chest. Everything he'd said had put her determination to leave him into disarray.

Falling for my secretary...

That barely there hint of regard shouldn't make her blood race, but it did.

"We've managed until now and we were furious with each other," he cajoled.

"I'm still furious," she interjected with more exasperation than heat. A lot of her bitter loathing was dissolving. She couldn't help it. Getting that peek into his past explained so much, not least his single-minded determination to succeed.

And it did nothing to dissipate the attraction she felt toward him. If anything, it was worse now. The thick walls she'd built against him were thinning and little fantasies of somehow finding a future with him, earning his trust and maybe his love, sparkled like fairy dust in the edges of her vision.

So dumb.

Given what he'd just told her, it was time to accept that he would never, ever love her. The best she could hope for was this, a truce and a fresh start.

Injustice sawed behind her breastbone like an abrasive file.

Lucy grew heavy in her arms. She started to change her position, then let Raoul take her, watching as the limp infant was tucked lovingly into her father's chest.

Folding her empty arms, she tried telling herself she could manage alone, but she couldn't ignore his point about day care.

"My mother wants to see her," Raoul added in quiet insistence. "You know how hard travel is on her. Lucy obviously hates the bottle. We could force the issue—"

"No!" she blurted, hating thinking of Lucy being distressed about anything. If she preferred to breast-feed, well, this was a finite time in both their lives.

"You'll come to New York with us, then."

"Don't start with your pushy tactics! I know how you work, getting a small concession and turning it into a major one," she said with mild disgust. "I'll *think* about New York. And if I go, it won't be as your—"

Lover? Mistress? Girlfriend? The words all sounded so superficial and temporary, paring her self-worth down to nothing.

"Nanny?" he prompted, mouth quirking briefly, then he sobered. "I'd have to hire one if you don't go. I'd prefer to pay you. You could quit the transcription."

"Don't make it sound easy. It's not."

One long masculine finger touched her jaw, turning her face to his. "What's hard? Making the promise about not stealing? Or keeping it?"

His challenge pinned her so she felt like an insect squirming in place, unable to escape even though she wanted to scamper away. Dying by increments, she felt the spasm of hurt reflect in her face before she was able to mask it, but a pierce of pain stayed lodged in her heart like an iron spike.

Looking him straight in the eye, she defiantly said, "I will never take anything from you. Ever."

He held her gaze for so long she almost couldn't stand it. Tightness gripped her chest and her skin felt too small for her body.

He nodded once.

As he walked away, she hung back, trembling. Had she lost or won?

Raoul's mother cried when she held Lucy for the first time.

"I never imagined he'd give me a grandchild. He's such a workaholic." Beatrisa was a tall, slender woman who dressed well and bound her silver hair into a figure eight behind her head. Her subtle makeup enhanced her aristocratic features and she wore elegant jewelry that Sirena suspected were gifts from her son.

Beatrisa had always seemed to lack a real spark of life and now Sirena understood why. She felt a tremendous need to be kind to the older woman, and was glad she'd conceded to the trip, even though everything about staying in this house was awkward.

"She thinks we're a couple," she hissed when they were given a room to share.

"What a crazy assumption, with the baby and all," he drawled.

"You should explain to her."

"How?" he countered with exasperation.

Oh, that attitude of his grated. Especially since she could see how it would go. Beatrisa was being incredibly polite, plainly trying not to pry as she accepted their "modern" relationship with a murmur about admiring independent women. Any attempt to clarify would crack open the marriage question and Raoul *didn't see any point in that.*

Not that she wanted to marry him. No, they might have found a truce and a crooked understanding with their revelations about their past, but it wasn't as though he'd magically fallen in love with her. For her part, she was too aware of how easily she could tip back into crazy infatuation with him, making her vulnerable to his dominant personality. He'd broken her heart once already. She couldn't let him do it again.

"I'll use the bed in Lucy's room," she said.

His sigh rang with male frustration. "The doctor cleared you for more than travel, didn't he?"

"So I'm supposed to fall into bed with you?" She swung around to glare at him across the foot of the enormous, inviting bed with its plump pillows and slippery satin cover. "I realize you think I slept with you to hide my crime, but sex isn't that mindless for me. I need feelings on both sides."

A chill washed over her as her words rang in her ears. Nausea threatened, the kind that came from deep mortification. She was an independent woman, all right, one whose only solace against her obsession with her boss was that he'd never known how deep it went, but she'd just snapped her way into humiliation. Her clothes might as well be on the floor around her ankles, she felt so naked and exposed.

He stood arrested, but the wheels were spinning fast behind his inscrutable stare.

Trying to stay ahead of any conclusions he might draw, she gathered her toothbrush and pajamas from her bag, aware she was shaking but unable to control it.

"Of course, I'm given to self-deception," she stammered. "And thank God, or we wouldn't have Lucy, would we? But we both know how we feel about each other now and I make enough fresh mistakes without having to repeat old ones, so…"

She practically ran from the room before locking herself into Lucy's, where she threw herself facedown on the bed and quietly screamed into a pillow.

CHAPTER NINE

RAOUL HAD GROWN up in New York, but he didn't care for
it. Too many dark memories. The climate didn't help, always socked in with rain or buried in snow or suffocat-
ingly humid with summer heat. The place forced on him a
heavy feeling of a weight inside him that he couldn't shift.

He was already struggling with that when he paused
on his way into a meeting and instructed the receptionist
to interrupt him if Sirena called.

"Ms. Abbott? I thought she'd left the company! How
is she?" The woman's warmth and interest were sincere.

His blunt "Fine" was rude. And a lie. He'd left the house
before he'd seen her this morning, but he knew from the
way Sirena had blanched last night that she was not fine.
He almost suspected she was injured in a way he hadn't
considered.

Brooding while he half listened to his engineers develop a workback schedule, he did some math. He hadn't
added everything together since their talk over drinks that
night by the pool because he'd been distracted by other
revelations, but if it was true she hadn't dated after that
boy in college, she'd had exactly one lover since her first,
ill-fated relationship.

Him.

*...sex isn't that mindless for me. I need feelings on
both sides.*

The way she'd practically grabbed the voice bubble from the air and gobbled it back indicated pretty clearly that she'd never meant to admit that to him. Which made it disturbingly sincere.

Of course, I'm given to self-deception, she'd added to cover up, but that only made him grind his teeth, wondering if he was as well. Despite her motives for stealing unfolding into a picture of a woman who hadn't believed he'd help if she asked, he'd never wavered from believing she'd slept with him to cover up what she'd done.

He needed to believe it. Anything else was too uncomfortable. He wasn't a womanizer. He didn't take advantage of the vulnerable. He didn't lead women on.

She hadn't expected one hookup to be a marriage proposal, she'd said, but had expected to be treated with respect.

At the time of their affair, he'd been way past respect into genuine liking. Affection. Something deeper he'd never contemplated letting himself feel.

God, when he thought back to how those twenty-four hours had gone, it was like another lifetime. The sweetness of her, the relief of finally giving in to touching her, the powerful release that had shaken him to the core...

The doors opening inside him, a sensation like footsteps invading the well-guarded depths of his soul. Even as their damp, half-clothed bodies had been trembling in ecstasy, he'd crashed back to the reality of what they'd just done. Whom he'd done it with. How vulnerable he felt.

His inner panels had lit up with alarm signals. While Sirena's plump lips had grazed his throat, he'd been withdrawing, deeply aware of a sense of jeopardy. His father hadn't killed himself because he'd fallen for his secretary. He'd killed himself because he'd *fallen.* In love. Deep emotions drove men to desperate acts.

What he'd felt for Sirena in those loaded minutes of sensual closeness had scared the hell out of him.

He'd pulled away, said something about the rain having stopped. By the time he'd dropped her at her building and returned to his own, he'd been primed for a reason, any reason, to knock her so far away from him she'd never reach him again.

And he had.

...Even my stepmother didn't go that far to hurt me.

Rather than killing himself, he'd destroyed what had been growing between them.

It was a sickening, horrid vision of himself. He lurched to his feet, needing to escape his own pathetic weakness, but only drew the attention of the room.

"Problem, sir?" The group stood back to look between him and the Smart Board where the schedule could have been written in Sanskrit for all the sense it made.

"I have to make a call," he lied, and strode through the maze of cubicles clattering with keyboard strikes into his office. It contained two desks, one that was a bold, masculine statement and the other a stylish work space that, for a time, had been the first place he glanced. Now it stood as a monument to his colossal overreaction.

He rubbed his face, hating to feel this tortured, this *guilty.* The fact remained, she had stolen from him, he reminded himself.

But he hadn't lashed out at her for that. She'd angered him, yes, but her real crime had been moving him in the first place. Sirena had dared to penetrate walls nobody else had dared breach.

Lust isn't caring.

No, it wasn't, but what he felt wasn't mere lust.

Sirena was grateful that Raoul had left for the office before she rose. Of course, she was also hypocrite enough to miss him despite her chagrin over her revelation last night. There was also envy and disgruntlement that he still worked in one of the many dynamic, ever-changing offices she had loved so much. Who had taken her place? She hated her usurper on principle.

Chatting with Beatrisa, hearing stories of Raoul's childhood became a nice distraction from her muddled emotions.

When he returned unexpectedly at lunch, it was with a surprise: tickets to a matinee. "Musicals aren't my speed. I'll stay with Lucy. You ladies have fun."

It was an incredible treat, the sort of thing Sirena used to wish for every time they visited New York, but had never found time or funds for. Afterward they had tea and scones in a glitzy café until Raoul texted that his daughter had inherited his stubborn streak.

Giggling over his self-deprecating assessment, they rushed back so Sirena could feed their starving baby. Full of excitement about their afternoon, she was disappointed when Raoul said, "I'm glad you enjoyed it. Start dinner without me. I have a call to make."

When he found his way to the table, he was wearing his cloak of remoteness. His mother didn't pick up the signals of his distraction, but Sirena did. While Beatrisa talked about their day, the feeling of being left out of his world struck Sirena afresh, but she supposed his turning aloof was better than another clash like last night's.

As Beatrisa wound down over coffee, Raoul finally said, "I'm afraid we've had a change of plans, Mother. We won't be able to stay the week. The company has been nominated for an award in L.A. I have to fly out to pick it up."

"You hate those things!" Sirena blurted. It had always been her job to figure out who could show up in his place, make the arrangements and prepare a speech.

"Surely you could do that without dragging Sirena and the baby across the country? They can stay here with me," his mother said.

Sirena shrugged. Lucy was out of sorts enough with the time change from London. She didn't need another one.

Raoul only gave his coffee cup a quarter turn and said, "They've specifically asked if Sirena would attend. It's that bunch we worked with for the special-effects software," he told her. "You always made an impression with my associates. You've been sorely missed by a lot of them."

Sirena flushed hot and cold, not sure how to respond. She missed everything about her job, but she couldn't go back to it, so she tried not to think of it.

As she considered all those beautiful women he'd taken to galas and cocktail parties, she also felt too inadequate to be his date. "I never attended that sort of thing with you before—" she started to dismiss.

"Things are different now, aren't they?"

How? She lifted a swift glance and collided with his unrelenting stare, like he was pushing his will upon her. She instinctively bristled while the fault line in her chest gaped and widened. "There's no one to watch Lucy."

"Miranda's agreed to fly in and sit with her."

"You want to fly your stepsister to L.A. to babysit?" It was ludicrous—and the way he briefly glanced away, as though he wasn't being honest with her, put her on guard.

"She flies all the time doing those trade shows. We'll need to leave early, but we'll come back here for a day or two on our way back to London." He rose, putting an end to the discussion in a completely familiar way.

Old habits of accommodating his needs collided with the newer ones of taking care of her baby's needs and her own. "Raoul."

"This is important to me, Sirena. Please don't argue."

Wow. Had he just said *please?* Shock struck her dumb long enough he was able to escape without her raising another argument.

By morning, it was too late. When he said early, he meant early, coming into her room to begin packing Lucy's things while shooing Sirena's sleepy head into the shower. Being naked and knowing he was just beyond the door made her senses flare, but he was completely indifferent. They were on the plane within the hour.

Lucy didn't enjoy the altitude climb, so they were well in the air before Sirena caught her breath. She gratefully embraced a cup of coffee while Raoul swept and tapped his way across a tablet screen.

"I liked that crew from the film, too, but I can't believe you shook us out of bed for them. What's really going on?" she asked.

"Use the stateroom if you want more sleep." He didn't even look up.

"No, I've had coffee now. You'll have to entertain me," she volleyed back.

His gaze came up with pupils so big his eyes were almost black. After a checking glance to their sleeping infant, he swung a loaded *"Okay"* to her.

In a blink, he'd transformed from the distracted man intent on his work that she'd seen a million times to a predatory male thinking of nothing but sex.

Her skin tightened and a flush of excitement flooded her with heat. Most betraying of all, tingles pooled in a swirl of sharp desire deep between her thighs.

His tense mouth eased into a smile of approval while he took a slow visual tour to her breasts, where her nipples stung with need. He didn't move, but suddenly he felt very close. He knew exactly what was happening to her.

She yanked her gaze away, but the picture of his masculine beauty stayed with her. The man had a chest to absolutely die for and she ached to see it again, run her hands over his smooth shoulders and taut abs.

Embarrassed by her shortened breath and prickling arousal, she swallowed and said a strangled, "I think we've covered that. It's not on."

Silence. And when she risked a glance at him, his jaw was clenched.

"Because you think I don't have feelings for you," he growled.

"I don't expect you to," she stated stiffly, then had to dip her face to stare into her empty mug, hiding that she was going red with indignity. "Obviously you've been very decent, taking me in when I was sick, but that was more to do with Lucy, wasn't it? And yesterday was nice, but it was a treat for your mother. Shows like that aren't your thing, you said. So you sent me, which isn't to say I didn't enjoy it, just that I realize it wasn't about me."

"You have a stellar opinion of me and my motives, don't you?"

"I'm not trying to insult you."

"You're doing a helluva job of it anyway. Let's hope this trip redeems me in your eyes." He went back to his tablet, shutting her out, which was probably a good thing.

He'd disconcerted her, sounding almost injured. A tiny worm of ambiguity niggled in her. Was she working so hard to protect herself she was failing to see the softer feelings she'd once been convinced were there? Or was that delusion a short trip to another painful tumble?

Despite the caffeine in her system, she wound up dozing and before she knew it, they were in California. They didn't stay in the suite they'd used two years ago, when he'd been working with the special-effects company. This was a new, ultrachic building designed on a curve, like a giant glass-and-bronze half cylinder with its back to the ocean.

Inside the penthouse, the floor-to-ceiling windows were framed in gray-and-white geometric squares. The tiles and carpet marked severe paths through the open plan of lounge, kitchen and dining area. All of the furniture was angular and modern, but luxury softened the hard edges. Jewel-colored pillows and billowy curtains gave it a sexy, romantic feel and the stunning three-sixty views to mountains and ocean and cityscape were breathtaking. Sirena's first thought was of the bath she'd take after dark, surrounded by the twinkling lights of the city.

As was her habit, she ran a brisk inventory as she explored, ensuring all the standard arrangements for Raoul were made.

"No Chivas and no cord for the secure internet connection." She adjusted the drapes in the main room to let in more of the brilliant sunshine and view of the ocean. "I'll call down. Did you want extra of that rain forest coffee you like to take home?"

He didn't answer, so she turned to see him watching her with a bemused expression. "I would love that, thank you."

His appreciation poured sunlight directly into her soul. A huge smile tried to take over her face and she had to turn away to hide how easily he flipped her inside out. What the hell was she doing? No way was she begging for a shred of affection. She needed to nip this craziness in the bud.

Fortunately their daughter woke and demanded attention, then a stylist showed up with a measuring tape and color swatches.

"What? Why?" Sirena argued as Raoul took the baby so she could lift her arms.

"We have that red carpet thing in a few nights," he reminded.

"You didn't say red carpet! I thought it was a cocktail party." She hadn't gained a ton of baby weight, she'd been too sick, but even though she'd started back on the treadmill, she was soft and had bags under her eyes. She'd never clean up like the stunners who usually hung off his arm.

Muddled and anxious, she got through the rest of the day and took some air on the balcony after her bath. A clean breeze off the water had swept away the pollution and the air smelled sultry, helping ease her unsettled mind.

Raoul joined her, making her stomach quiver in awareness. She ignored it.

"What do you think? Should I buy this unit?" he asked her.

"They're treating you to entice you?" she guessed, then rejected the luxurious surroundings with a haughty shake of her head. "I came out here to see the fireworks over the happiest place on earth and I don't, so it's no good. A major disappointment."

"I'll make the purchase contingent on their moving the building to the next county," he drawled.

"Ha!" She laughed at herself. "I guess I should look at a map. It's just always been on my bucket list to come to L.A., visit the theme parks, wear the ears…I thought I'd at least see the castle and fireworks while I'm here."

"You can. We'll be here a week. Take—" He cut himself off.

"Lucy isn't old enough to appreciate it," she scoffed, predicting what he had almost said. "No, I can wait for another time." To avoid his casually rumpled masculine appearance, she looked to the glowing blue of the pool jutting off to the right on their patio, a few steps down. It was surrounded by orange trees in oversized planter pots and twined with pinpoints of white lights. "If we come here again."

She pursed her lips, wondering if this would become her life. She suspected so and took a second to self-examine.

"Honestly, Raoul? I don't know if I would have enjoyed the travel half so much if we'd been staying at cheap motels and taking shuttle buses through dodgy back alleys. You live very well. It makes me very tempted to stay with you indefinitely."

"That's the only thing that tempts you?" he asked with mild disgust.

"Oh, please! You're not that insecure." She was glad it was dark and he couldn't see how she took in his physique with a swift glance and a hard blush. "You could drive shuttle buses for back-alley hotels and still be appealing. But I've been in a relationship for practical reasons. They aren't as great as they look. I knew from the outset I wouldn't be with Stephan forever and it made me feel trapped. I don't want to start something unless I know we can both live with it for a very long time."

"I hate hearing you talk about him." He gave her a pointed look that landed like a spear in her heart, sticking and vibrating. "This is the least practical or convenient relationship I've ever been in, but I still want it. I want *you.*"

"You mean you—"

"Don't," he interrupted, stepping so close she pressed back into the rail.

She gripped it, heart zooming into flight as his potent masculinity clouded around her like a spell. "Don't what?"

"Don't say I only want my daughter. I do, but that's not why I'm out here. I saw you walk by with this robe clinging to your damp skin…" His nostrils flared as he seared his glance down her front. One hand came out to hook into her belt, tugging lightly.

She should have let him draw her forward, but she resisted and the belt gave way.

Something flared in his silver eyes.

"Raoul." She meant it as a protest, but it was more an enticing whisper.

"Let me," he growled, and with slow deliberation parted

the edges of her robe. She was naked beneath and he swore softly before murmuring, "You're so beautiful."

She desperately needed to hear that. No one ever complimented her and seeing the way he ate up her figure was intensely gratifying, filling up a hollow part of her soul.

The cool night air made her skin pimple, knotting her nipples into tight buds and swirling to the warm places on her abdomen and thighs. A suffusion of heat followed, one incited by the hunger and admiration in his long study of her nude body.

"Raoul," she moaned again, this time on a helpless whimper.

He groaned and stepped closer, shod feet bracketing her bare ones. His hot hands sought her waist and circled to her back, pulling her into contact with his clothed body.

She let her head fall back and met his open mouth with her own, moaning at how wrong this was, but she wanted it so badly. Her hands eased their death grip on the rail and rose to stroke over his shoulders, following the rippling flex of his shoulder blades as he swooped his hands over the small of her back, cupped her naked bottom and pressed her aching pelvis into firm contact with the ridge of his erection.

There was no buildup, no mental debate as she wondered if her desire would catch. Everything about this man turned her switches on. All he had to do was touch her. Her hips tilted, seeking more intimate contact with his hardness.

He thrust his tongue into her mouth in a bold claim, cupping the side of her face to hold her for his devastating kiss. She pulled him into her, wanting more, loving the stroke of his restless hands, the way he clasped her breast and gently crushed and massaged and softly bit her lips before he lifted his head.

"Bedroom," he said, starting to pull her with him.

She came to her senses and pressed a hand to his chest. "We can't."

"Why not?"

For the life of her, she couldn't think of anything but feeling him inside her, but that's all it would be. Physical feelings. For him. As much as she wanted the release, she knew she'd never be able to keep it that dispassionate.

As he read her rejection, his expression shuttered. With a feral noise, he lurched away and grasped the rail to the lower balcony and vaulted to the pool deck below.

"What—?"

He landed between a pair of loungers, took three long strides and dove straight into the pool.

Sirena slapped a hand over her mouth, astonished as she watched his blurred image move with surprising speed down the length of the pool, all underwater. He was halfway back before he rose to gasp for air.

"What on earth are you doing?" she cried.

"What the hell are you doing?" he shot back, kicking himself to the far edge and hefting himself onto the ledge. Yanking at his wet shirt, he struggled out of it and dropped it beside his hip with a splat. "Get inside or I'm coming after you and this time I'm not stopping."

She spun and ran to her room, where she hugged a pillow and told herself she'd made the right decision.

Even though it felt like the stupidest choice in the world.

"Sirena!"

It was about time. Odious man. First he made her so crazy she spent the night hating herself for not sleeping with him when she would have hated herself more if she *had*. Then he left without writing a note, giving no indication of where he was going or when to expect him back—although he had prepared the coffee machine so all she had to do was push the button. But that didn't excuse barging in here, yelling her name when she was trying to settle their daughter.

"Sirena, where—? Oh, here you are."

She glared at him. "She was almost asleep." She lightly bounced the baby to ease her drowsy eyes closed again.

"I'll take her," he said, moving forward in that battle-ship way of his.

"Fine, take her. Maybe she'll sleep for you," she muttered, grouchy because she needed a nap as badly as the baby. Maybe going to bed with him *now....*

Shut up, Sirena.

"I don't want you to drop her," he said, "when you see who I brought with me."

She sidestepped to see a young woman in the doorway. She was blonde, slender, achingly sweet-looking in her innocent way, yet tall and curvy without a hint of the preadolescent she'd been the last time Sirena had seen her.

Allison's soft brown eyes pooled with giant tears while a great, mischievous grin widened her mouth. She thrust out her arms. "Me," she burst out. "Surprise!"

A scream built in Sirena's throat and locked it, making pressure expand so hard her eyes filled. She choked, try-ing to gasp a breath, and began to shake. She wanted to move forward, but her knees started to sag.

Raoul caught her, swearing under his breath. "I should have warned you, but I didn't want to build expectations if anything went wrong—"

"It's okay, it's okay," she babbled, wanting to lean into him, but forcing her legs to take her weight. She passed through a thick mist that was pure sparkle and magic. As she reached the familiar yet very grown-up sister she hadn't seen in the flesh for so long, she realized her cheeks hurt because she was smiling bigger than she ever had in her life.

"You don't look this tall when we talk on my tablet,"

she managed to joke even as a sobbing laugh rattled her voice. Her arms wrapped around her baby sister.

Ali's wiry embrace crushed her. The physical contact was so deeply moving, Sirena thought she'd break into pieces.

The women held on to each other a long time, making Raoul's throat close. Ali, as she had said she liked to be called, had chattered excitedly in the limo, her gestures and tone oddly Sirena-like despite the faint accent and fair coloring. She had a measure of Sirena's steely core, too. When he'd asked why her parents hadn't come, she'd only said, "Mum can be funny sometimes," and lifted her chin. He had the impression this trip was a bit of rebellion and wondered if it would have repercussions for Sirena.

He'd found Faye oddly obstructive, considering he was offering an all-expenses-paid trip to America. It had been hard to sidestep her demand to speak to Sirena, which he suspected might have called off Ali's visit.

Navigating future altercations with Sirena's family was a concern for another time, he decided. This moment, seeing how happy he'd made Sirena, was worth any trouble down the road.

The women pulled back to stare at one another, glowing in an aura of happiness.

Ali's gaze dragged toward him. "Can I meet Lucy? I've been dying to hold her." She took her niece and sighed with adoration. "Oh, Sin, she's beautiful."

Sin, he silently repeated, liking the nickname immediately.

"Isn't she?" she agreed shamelessly. Eyes damp and lips trembling, she cupped her flushed cheeks in her hands.

She looked so taken aback and overwhelmed Raoul couldn't help moving toward her, but he was almost afraid to touch her. She seemed to be struggling to contain her emotions. Gently he smoothed her hair back from the side of her face. "I didn't realize this would be such a shock. Are you all right?"

She flashed him one glimpse of the naked emotions brimming in her, then threw herself at him.

He took the hit of her soft weight with a surprised "Oof," then closed his arms around her.

She buried her face in the middle of his chest, clinging tightly, barely audible as she said, "You have no idea what this means to me. I can't ever thank you enough."

All the sexual heat of last night's embrace came back as he felt the press of her breasts and was surrounded in her feminine scent of green tea and pineapple. An incredible wash of tenderness accompanied it. He had wanted to do something nice, but had never suspected such a small thing would have such magnificent impact.

Governed by instinct, he enfolded her and stroked her hair. His chin caressed her silky locks and he had to swallow the emotion from his throat. He'd forgotten this perk in letting yourself feel for another person. When they were happy, you were happy. He should have done this sooner. He'd healed a crack in her heart, filled it with joy, and it had taken nothing. A couple of phone calls and a plane ticket. What did that say about how lonely she'd been?

"You two," Ali trilled. "You're so cute."

Sirena realized she was all over Raoul like a coat of paint. After last night she didn't know where they stood. She always felt this pull around him and at this moment felt positively anchored to him, heart to heart. Misreading their connection had gotten her where she was today, though.

Pulling away, she swiped her fingertips under her eyes, trying to get a grip. Her overwhelmed emotions weren't just shock and joy over seeing her sister. There was a huge part shaken to the core that Raoul had done this for her. She tried to remind herself that the cost was nothing to him, but to think of it and make it happen…

Did he feel something for her after all?

She was afraid to look at him, fearful of seeing nothing and being disappointed. She was also terrified that her shields were so far gone he'd see right into her soul and the special place she reserved for him beside it.

"This is like Christmas," she said, clearing her throat and searching for a stronger voice. "It really puts to shame that tie I haven't even bought Raoul."

They all laughed and the day became a celebration, California-style. Raoul ordered brunch and mimosas and joined them on and off as they sat by the pool, taking turns holding Lucy and catching up.

By evening, the excitement and time change had caught up to all of them and they had an early night. The next morning, she met Raoul in the kitchen.

"Can't sleep?" she said with an attack of nerves, feeling defenseless without Lucy or Ali to still the sexual vibrations that immediately flared between them. "Me, either."

"I have a heavy morning before everyone in Europe goes home, but I wanted to give you these." He showed her some tickets. "I almost spilled the beans about Ali when you were talking about this the other night. I came this close to suggesting you take her."

Sirena gasped as she caught sight of the iconic fairy circling the castle with dust. "Raoul!"

"For the record, these are not for her, although I hope she enjoys the day as much as you do. These aren't for Lucy either." The bright tickets came alongside her jaw as he crooked his finger under her chin, making her lift her eyes to his. "These are for you, because it's something you've always wanted."

He kissed her. The gesture was so sweet she couldn't help clinging to his lips with her own. His taste made goose bumps lift all over her body.

She swallowed and tried to hide how touched she was

by joking, "I really don't know what to think of all this." Her heart rate picked up, daring to conjecture there might be a hint of tenderness or affection driving him after all. "You're going to a lot of trouble just to keep things *in-house*."

"Sirena—" His quick, defensive blurt of her name made her wave a quick hand.

"I'm sorry. I'm being cheeky because I don't know what else to say, not because I think you have ulterior motives," she hurried to excuse.

He sighed. "I realize I'm not demonstrative." Leaning near the sink, he studied her, his body language heavy. A range of emotions ran across his usually stoic face. They were intimate and, she suspected, indicative of deep scarring.

She instantly wanted to reach out with reassurance, but felt too shy and uncertain so she wound up standing there with her hands wringing, the silence thick and awkward. What could she say anyway? That a couple of kisses and nice gestures had won her over? They hadn't. She had tons of misgivings.

He ran a hand over his face. "After my father, I pushed everyone to a safe distance. What he'd done was too cruel. He was a good man, a good father. We played catch, went fishing. It was a perfect childhood. I'll never understand why he killed himself or how anyone could say they love someone and hurt them that badly. Letting down my guard with anyone since then…it's not something that's comfortable for me."

Outwardly she handled what he was saying, taking it on the chin without flinching, even though she was screaming inside. Even though she was pretty sure she paled and her bones turned to powder. Somehow she stayed there, nodding circumspectly, saying, "I understand."

Her words seemed to hurt him. He winced.

"No, I do," she assured, being as honest as he was. "I have my own baggage that makes me worry you'll pull up stakes without a moment's notice. It makes me scared to let things move to…" She swallowed, trying to find a description that wouldn't reveal too much. "To a level of deeper dependence."

"I'm not going anywhere. This is everything I want, right here." He pointed to the floor between them, suggesting the domesticity of waking every morning with her and their little family, which was nice, but it wasn't the fairy tale on the tickets.

She had to let go of that. Better to keep her expectations realistic even if it hurt. And it hurt so much to know he would never love her. Not the way she loved him.

Oh. The knowledge of how deep her feelings had become went through her like a sweet, potent potion. This wasn't infatuation with the boss. It wasn't hormones raging for the wrong man. It was the evolution of feelings and attraction she'd always felt toward him. They had tumbled into deep devotion and longing to make a life with him.

Swallowing the lump that came into her throat, she hid her angst with a smile. "Even though you seem to do everything and I haven't done one thing for you? How about breakfast, at least?" She turned her back on him as she peered into the refrigerator, defusing the charged moment.

The spoiling didn't stop, however. After their day at the park, he appalled the upscale clientele of a rooftop restaurant by daring to bring a baby, of all things, into their exclusive establishment. They saw the fireworks from their table, of course. A trip to the beach was arranged the next day and a drive along the coastline the following. They lunched on fresh seafood and local wines and scouted art studios for bargains.

Then the preparations for the technology awards started.

Raoul escorted them into a design house on Rodeo Drive and handed over his credit card to a stylist.

"Ali, find some things for yourself and if you see something your mother would like, put that on there too. I'm having a prototype of my new gadget flown in for your father. You can take that back for him, but if you see something for him…" He leaned to kiss Sirena's cheek, trailing off as he prepared to take his leave.

"Dad's tastes are pretty simple," she said blankly, startled by his casual affection. He'd been so solicitous these last few days, a hand often finding its way to the middle of her back or resting at her waist, but she still wasn't used to it.

"Whatever you think is best. I'll be at Armani, having my tux fitted. Because I need another one." He rolled his eyes. "I'll come back for Lucy when I'm done."

They seated Ali in an overstuffed armchair and offered her champagne. Sirena leaned down to give her Lucy so she could have her fitting and Ali whispered, "It's like we're living *Pretty Woman*. You're going to marry him, right?"

"Sweetie, I keep telling you, it's not like that. We just had a moment that got us into a situation and we're trying to make the best of it." She didn't know how else to explain her circumstances without revealing details that were far from romantic.

Back when she'd been pregnant and under suspicion, she'd kept the arrest from her family. It hadn't been her father's fault, but he would have felt responsible. She certainly didn't want her sister feeling guilty about pursuing her teaching dream.

Now, well, she didn't want to tell Ali everything for fear she'd think badly of Raoul. The things Raoul had shared with her were deeply personal and without being able to balance his actions against his motives, he would look like a cold, unforgiving monster. Which was miles from the truth.

Sighing a little, she had to admit he was actually what she'd always admired him for being: a strong, ambitious man with a deep streak of responsibility and loyalty to his family. He was gallant after growing up around women, innately desiring to protect and provide for his own. Even if he had been toothless, dirt-poor and overweight, he'd still open doors and show incredible patience for women who couldn't decide which shoes or lipstick to wear. He'd still walk a baby all night and start the coffee for her mother.

And she'd still love him.

"Oh, Sin, you're gorgeous," Ali murmured as Sirena walked back to her.

With a pinch in her heart, she studied the emerald gown and thought about how she was the complete opposite of Raoul. She could dress up in world-class finery, have her teeth whitened, love their baby and he'd still only see her as a thief.

CHAPTER TEN

RAOUL WENT IN search of Sirena, hearing Ali saying with exasperation, "She'll be fine. We both will. I swear."

"But call if you need to. Or text. You have Raoul's number if I don't hear mine?"

Suppressing a grin, he stepped into the doorway of the room operating as their nursery. Vaguely aware of Ali efficiently changing his daughter's nappy, he caught an eyeful of Sin and felt as though his breath had been punched out of him.

She had her back to him, but he was transfixed. He took in the curls pulled away from one ear to cascade like a waterfall over her opposite shoulder. Her off-the-shoulder gown in gypsy-green dipped to reveal one shoulder blade. A cutout on the other side offered a peek of her waist and spine. The skirt draped gracefully over her rounded hips to puddle sumptuously behind her. Distantly, he realized he wasn't getting any air, and that she hadn't even turned around, but she'd stolen his breath.

"Your date is here. Quite a dish, too," Ali said, cocking her chin in his direction.

He barely noticed the girl as the woman turned. Her plump bottom lip was caught in her teeth while her mossy eyes were pools of uncertainty. Always beautiful, Sirena didn't need makeup and the stylist had known it, only enhancing her stunning bone structure and opulent lashes with a streak of frosted jade and shimmering gold.

A wink of emeralds dangled from her ears and encircled her wrist. They were loaners, but he decided to buy them. They matched her eyes too perfectly to allow them to go to any other woman.

"I'm sorry," she said faintly. "Have you, um, been waiting for me?"

All my life.

"Get her out of here," Ali said with a nudge into Sirena's back. "She's being a nervous Nellie even though I keep telling her I babysat all of Sydney until I finally got a proper job at the real estate office."

Raoul held out his arm, not trusting his voice to tell her how beautiful she looked, then winced as she got there first, saying, "You look nice."

Her light touch curled into the curve of his elbow and a subtle mix of aromas filled his senses with floral and berry notes underscored with tangy citrus and a mysterious anise.

He waited until they were in the elevator, where he let the doors close without choosing a floor, before he gave in to temptation and reached to adjust the drape of her gown, revealing her leg and a shoe with a dominatrix heel.

"What are you doing?" She started to step her foot back inside the skirt, but he set a hand on the bared skin of her waist.

"Don't move, *Sin.*"

She gasped, cocking her hip to escape his touch as though it burned, but the flush of color that flooded under her skin and the spark that invaded her glistening eyes told him it was a more erotic reaction.

"You look amazing," he murmured as he removed his phone from his breast pocket.

Her eyes widened in surprise and her wicked mouth

twitched before she screened her thoughts behind a tangled line of mink. "Really?" She settled into a pose with the confidence of a woman who knew she looked her best and was having fun with it. Her shoulders went back, her breasts came up, her hips slanted and her feet parted just far enough to be provocative. "Men are so predictable."

She tossed her hair and offered a screen-legend smile.

"It's true," he agreed, snapping the photo. "We're simple creatures. Now take it off."

She laughed and hit the button for the lobby. "I'm keeping it on at least as long as it took me to get into it. Let me see." Her cool fingers grazed his in a soft caress as she urged him to slant the screen of his phone.

As he studied the photo with her, he saw what he hadn't meant to reveal. He'd liked the way the mirror showed the back of the gown and had angled the frame to catch it, but he hadn't noticed his own expression was caught in the reflection. Lust tightened his face. He wasn't ashamed of it, but his expression held something else.

He tucked the phone away, not wanting to examine the naked emotion on his face.

Discomfited, Sirena told herself she ought to be used to Raoul's mercurial moods, switching from warm familiarity to all business in the space of a heartbeat. With a pang near her heart, she tried to calm her racing pulse and quit building this into something it wasn't. But Ali's romantic nature was contagious. *He's going to propose. Why else does a man go to all this trouble?*

Ali didn't realize this level of luxury wasn't trouble for Raoul. It was completely normal and he probably took photos of all his dates, inserting them into his iLittleBlackBook so he could keep track of who was who.

The biting thought was wiped clear by another and she cringed inwardly. She really was the most misguidedly devoted ex-PA if she had to bite back remarking to him, *You know what might be a cool idea for an app?*

She was trying so hard to ground out her electric excitement she didn't realize the elevator doors had opened onto the opulent lobby.

"What's wrong?" he prompted.

Idiot. Trying to make light of her distraction, she quoted Julia Roberts under her breath. "If I forget to tell you later, I had a nice time tonight."

He didn't get it. In his typically classy fashion, he said very sincerely, "So did I."

Oh.

Her bones went soft as she took the hand he offered and let him lead her to the limo. It was like sitting down to an IMAX film where scenery rushing by became more intense and colorful, pulling her into a surreal world she had seen from a distance before, but that now drew her in three dimensionally.

Bulbs went off as they walked the red carpet. Action stars were everywhere and this wasn't even a big awards show. *Just Hollywood indulging itself,* Raoul had said. Still she could hardly keep her jaw from dropping.

The show was a pageantry of talent, one woman's singing almost bringing Sirena to tears. During a break, Raoul said, "You're really enjoying this."

"How could I not? I don't have any natural talents of my own, so I'm in complete awe of those that do."

"You're an excellent mother, Sirena."

"Oh, please," she deflected, uncomfortable with flattery. "Having a baby nearly killed me and I'm bumbling my way through colic and feeding. I'm hardly gifted."

"Don't joke about that," he said with gravity. "Ever."

Like all criticisms, deserved or not, she took his remark to heart and hid her abraded soul by sitting straight, chin level. His category was called next anyway, putting an end to the short conversation.

He won, of course, which was well deserved. As he rose, he clasped her hand and tried to bring her up with him.

"No!" she said, horrified. Her emotions were right there under the surface, barely contained. She wasn't standing under massive lights when she was this close to tears.

Setting his mouth into a displeased line, he went to the podium and waited for the applause to die down.

"This innovative software came out of a need for a specific effect. It wouldn't have been developed if not for the people who demanded it. But I think the entire team will agree that we wouldn't have delivered on time, on budget without the support of my exceptional assistant at the time, Sirena Abbott. She refused to come on stage with me because she's more comfortable in a supporting role than in the spotlight. I've come to realize that about you, Sin."

The nickname was a tiny endearment, but the intensity of his gaze picking her out across the crowded auditorium was monumental. Later she would realize heads and cameras had turned her way, but in this moment, all she saw and felt was Raoul's undivided attention.

"You recently did the hard work on a very special project in which I played a very small role. I won't take credit for the beautiful baby girl you made us. If we were giving golden statues for that tonight, this would be yours."

Now her makeup was going to run, vexing man! She blinked, trying to hold back the tears.

He was escorted offstage by handlers for photos. He'd warned her that would happen and she gratefully grasped the chance to slip into the ladies' room to collect herself. No one had ever made such a production of appreciating her. She didn't know how to cope with it. Criticism was hurtful, but she was comfortable with it. She knew what to do after receiving it. The path to Better was right there and she always took it.

Arriving at Well Done made her look around in confusion. Part of her wanted to dismiss what Raoul had said as empty flattery, but she knew that wasn't healthy and she loved their daughter too much to reduce the sweet things he'd just said about her, even if that meant accepting praise for her own contribution.

She *did* try to be a good mother and a good person. Was it so far-fetched that he might have noticed and come to value those things about her?

With her breath still hitching, she left the ladies' room and ran straight into Raoul. He was clutching his award in one fist as he paced. He stopped when he saw her.

"I was about to come in there looking for you."

"Shoes and a dress like this are challenging," she joked to hide her discomfiture.

Someone else came into the short hallway and he nudged her farther into the moderate privacy of an area where a bank of outdated pay telephones still hung. That was the millionth time he'd stroked his fingers over the bare skin at her waist and it was totally short-circuiting her brain.

"Are you upset with me?" he asked.

"For what?" She ducked her head to the snap on her pocketbook, not wanting him to see how gauche she felt, unable to take one little compliment.

"For telling the world we have a baby together."

"Oh. That." She pressed her freshly painted lips together, mouth quirking wryly. "It's not the way I would have done it, but I'm not going to pretend she doesn't exist."

"It's not the way I meant to reveal her either. I was fielding some awkward questions backstage about whether we're getting married. It made me realize we should. Then you wouldn't worry about whether you could depend on me."

Stunned, Sirena could only stare at his bow tie, eyes burning as she reflected that it was even less sentimental than Stephan's awkward "Maybe we should get married."

"And before you accuse me of saying it purely for practicality's sake—" He clunked his heavy award onto a shelf and crowded her into a corner. "Let me remind you there's a reason we wound up with an unplanned pregnancy."

There went that hand again, possessively sliding to the small of her back, fingers dipping behind silk as he curved her into him, bumping her thighs into his.

She automatically caught at his sleeve for balance, but her other hand braced her pocketbook into his shoulder. Her head fell back a little, lips parting on a shocked gasp as her entire front lit up with seeking tingles, wanting contact with his.

"Fresh lipstick," she managed as his mouth neared hers.

"I don't care." He pressed hard lips over her trembling ones, both soothing and inciting the ache spreading through her body. Heat rose like a circle of flames around them, burning her alive as they pressed together, spinning and hurtling directly into the sun.

She groaned and met his tongue with hers, lifting on tiptoes to increase the pressure and even diving her fingers into his short hair to pull him down, urging him to kiss her harder. He did, rocking his mouth on hers with feral hunger. Hard fingers dug into her buttock and spine as he crushed her to him.

His erection imprinted her through the fabric of his pants, making the ethereal layer of silk gown seem nonexistent. She didn't want it between them. She wanted to feel nothing but satin skin over hard flesh, flexing muscle and the slam of his heartbeat against hers. She whimpered, almost sobbing in her need for him.

Drawing back a fraction, he muttered, "This is crazy." He had a hand tangled in her hair, clenching a handful in a way that kept her immobile. It would have been too cave-man and primitive if he wasn't also holding her as if he was saving her from a shipwreck and dropping hot kisses down the side of her face to her nape.

She trembled, mortified by how close she was to losing it in public. It was no consolation that he had her buried in a corner. People were coming and going behind him. They had to be glancing this way. Her hands had burrowed beneath his jacket, but they were flexing on his shirt, try-ing to pull it from his waistband so she could stroke the indent of his spine.

"Raoul, we have to stop."

"I know. I'm about to drag you into a janitor's closet." He straightened and pulled his snowy handkerchief from his pocket. He swiped it across his mouth, then asked her with a look if he'd gotten all the color off.

She thumbed a tiny smudge from the corner of his mouth and stole the cloth for herself, thinking to take it into the ladies' room, but he caught her hand and his award and started for the exit.

"What—?"

"Don't make me pick you up, Sin."

"I have a feeling you just did," she mumbled and heard him chuckle as he snapped for a limo.

"That one's not ours," she said.

"Ours will find us when we're ready," he assured her and had them driven about four blocks to the palatial entrance of a hotel. Throwing his platinum card on the counter, he got them a key in record time and seconds later they were walking into the decadence of the honeymoon suite.

Sirena stopped a few steps in, wondering what she was doing. It was one thing to be swept away, quite another to book a room and take off her clothes with deliberation.

Raoul unbuttoned his tuxedo jacket, shrugging out of it and throwing it across the arm of a wingback chair. "Second thoughts? I've had a vasectomy, if that's what you're worried about."

"What?" Her pocketbook hit the floor before she realized her fingers had released it. She quickly crouched to retrieve it, but couldn't take her eyes off the man with his hands pushed into tight fists in his trouser pockets. "When?"

"About a week after we fought about it. You asked if I'd pulled a hamstring on the treadmill and I said, 'something like that.'"

"You should have said—" She was floored, unable to process it. "Why would you do that? I'm a fluke. Other women—"

"I don't think about having sex with other women. Only you."

Her heart stumbled and she had a hard time rising to stand on her weak knees.

"I have condoms, too." He extracted a length of conjoined foil squares from his pocket. "In case you're worried about anything else. I've been tested and have never, ever not used one of these. Which frankly makes me nervous of my performance without one, given it's been so long since we were together."

Her mouth opened. Her lips and tongue wanted to form words, but no air moved from her throat. Her voice had left the building. He hadn't been with anyone else?

"We're good together, Sin." He crossed to her with a laconic scuff of his shoes on the tiles. "Even without taking this to the bedroom. We always were."

"Because I did as I was told," she managed to counter.

He took her chin, forcing her to look into his eyes. Her hair practically lifted off her scalp at his touch. His nearness and the way he studied her mouth caused her breath to stutter.

"I can't stand being around idiots or sycophants or

women who act helpless. You're bright and funny and incredibly competent. I've always been as attracted to that as the knockout body and gypsy looks."

Her lips began to quiver. "I still feel like anything could happen and it would all fall apart and you'd hate me again."

A sharp spasm seemed to take him. "You know what I hate? Not having you in my life at all. Oh, hell, don't cry. There's a lot to build on here, Sin."

"I know," she murmured, fingering the tail of his bow tie, wishing she had the courage to boldly yank it free. "Not to mention how much it would mean to me that Lucy would never wind up with a stepmother like my own."

His bearing hardened before her eyes, taking umbrage.

"Oh, please, you don't really need to hear that's not my only motive. I've been insanely attracted to you for years."

"I do need to hear that," he said with a tight white line around his mouth. "I need to hear it, see it, *feel* it…"

When he covered her mouth with his, the passion behind his kiss was cataclysmic. If she had wanted to be swept away, the tsunami of desire was here, lifting her so she found herself clutched to his chest and carried to the bed. But there an odd, intent stillness took him over. Everything slowed.

He sat beside her to run light fingers from her bare shoulder to her wrist, lifting her hand to his mouth. Hot, damp lips pressed into the thin skin of her inner arm, following the faint blue line to the crease of her elbow.

She compulsively wove her fingers into his silky hair, enjoying the play of the short strands on the sensitive spaces between her fingers. He smelled faintly of aftershave and firmly of himself. The compelling scent overwhelmed her as he nuzzled the hollow of her shoulder, then grazed his lips over the upper swell of her breast.

His shirt was a crisp annoyance as she sought the heat

beneath his collar, restricted by the tight buttons and bow tie and his refusal to crush her under his weight.

"I want to feel you," she complained, restively scraping her fingers up from his waistband to free his shirt, crumpling the fine silk.

He sat up. His narrow eyes glittered with something smug and arrogant, but his movements were urgent as he pulled at his clothing.

He does need to hear it, she thought, even as she rose on an elbow and picked at his buttons, trying to hurry him. As he threw off the shirt, she stroked across the twitching muscles of his chest, lightly scratching with her nails as she stroked from his collarbone to his abs.

"You're so hot," she breathed, thinking, *figuratively and literally.* He epitomized an underwear model's fine physique, but radiated heat from his swarthy, flush-darkened torso. His pure male sexuality weakened her. She was glad she was lying down, but a distant part of her was flinching in alarm. She'd done this once, stroked and satisfied her curiosity and his libido, and the next day her world had been devastated.

"Every time you clip up your hair, I want to let it down," he said in a sensuous rumble, gently seeking pins to release the hair pulled back from her temple. As he finger-combed, he bent to let his hot breath tease the delicate whorls of her ear. "I think of you doing very erotic things to me with this hair," he said, words and lips sensitizing her to screaming pitch before he took her to a new level of shivering excitement, dabbing his tongue and lightly biting and sucking her lobe. By the time he moved to the flesh at her nape, she was head-to-toe goose bumps, forehead pleated in an agony of delicious excitement. He further paralyzed her with soft bites into the incredibly responsive tendons of her neck, making her moan and arch to offer herself.

"What are you doing to me?" she gasped, making no

protest as he slid her wrists upward and clasped them in one of his hands.

"I haven't even got your dress off," he husked, seeking and finding the zip at her side. Slowly he released it, watching her pant as she waited, completely absorbed, wanting nothing except to belong to this man.

"You're like a goddess. A fantasy coming true, making me insane. I can't think of anything but having you." He released his grip on her to peel the one shoulder down her arm, exposing her breasts and avidly looking at them.

"Raoul." She brought her elbows down and forward, forearms wanting to shield herself, but his undisguised desire was a type of seduction. A deep part of her wanted to please him and if the thrust of her breasts excited him, she wanted to give him that.

He clasped the full globes in splayed hands and anointed them with reverent kisses. "So beautiful. So perfect." His hands slid to push the fabric down further and she lifted her hips, letting him take the gown off her legs, leaving her naked but for her slutty shoes and a nude thong that wasn't any kind of cover.

She'd been waxed, plucked, exfoliated and moisturized today, but she still held her breath, fearful he'd make note of her imperfections.

He chuckled with gruff pleasure and drew a wickedly teasing fingertip over the silk covering her hot and pulsing mound. His sure hands skimmed away that defense and suddenly she was painfully aware of wearing only shoes on a broad bed while she writhed in arousal before a half-dressed man.

"Raoul."

She didn't know what she wanted to say, but he said, "Shh," with quiet command.

His brows lowered in concentration as he cupped her hip in one hand, stilling her. His other hand moved to smooth a testing fingertip over her C-section scar. It was the starkest mark left by childbearing, even more pronounced than the faint stretch marks and the fading brown line descending from her belly button.

"Don't," she said, wriggling self-consciously and trying to brush his hand away.

"Tender?"

The scar was oddly both oversensitive and numb, but mostly his touch felt too personal. He bent to touch a kiss there and she gasped, shocked and moved and flooded with embarrassed excitement.

Then he shifted to blow softly over her mound. He'd been seducing her so gently, she'd overlooked how powerful and forceful he really was. Her contracting thighs smoothly parted for his superior strength as he made room for his wide shoulders, settling low to press licking kisses high on the insides of her legs.

"You don't have to…"

"Oh, sweet, hot Sin, I do. I really, really do."

She clenched her eyes shut as knowing fingers caressed. This was the sort of intimacy she'd never been able to relax for, knowing he was looking at her— *Oh, God.* Her muscles clenched on the finger that slid in to test her slippery depths.

"Tell me when I get it right," he said, taking a soft bite of her flesh. At the same time he withdrew his touch, then filled her with the span of two thick fingers. His tongue flicked and she couldn't bite back her keening moan. Everything in her gathered to this one bundle of pure sensation, paradise beckoning with each languid caress that he lazily bestowed on her, as if they had all the time in the world.

It was pure torture and so good she was dying, losing herself, growing wanton, inviting more with a tilt of her hips, encouraging him in gasps of sobbing murmurs.

"I can't take it," she cried, pulling mercilessly at his hair.

He reared back onto his knees with a near-primal growl, making her wail with loss even though she'd forced the issue.

Jerking at his trousers, he freed himself, shoving them off and away before he crawled over her. Her legs instinctively twined up to hitch her ankles behind his waist, trying to draw him down as he clasped the sides of her face and kissed her, hard.

His weight settled, crushing her pelvis before he lifted to allow her seeking hand to clasp his sleek shaft and guide him into her.

He slid home with a delicious plunge that turned his whole body to granite. For a few seconds he was a blistering, immovable cage around her, mouth locked to her lips, his heart the only movement as it pounded the wall of his chest, trying to reach hers.

A sigh of pure bliss left her. It felt so good to have him in her, filling the hollow ache she'd thought would be with her the rest of her life.

Then he eased back, pulling at her nerve endings as though they were harp strings, drawing her taut with ecstatic tension before he thrust again. Joy expanded within her.

The crescendo built, both of them clasping to be closer even as they fought to make the strokes harder, deeper, more irrevocable. This wasn't just her, she knew distantly. He was as lost to need as she was, clawing for satisfaction as if their lives depended on it. It did. She needed this, him, the raw hunger and the sweet struggle and the fight to hold on, hold back, to never let this end, to give and take...

The pinnacle arrived, holding them balanced on its tip, breath caught as they swayed between anguish and joy.

Elation won, tumbling them into the maw. He crushed

her as he throbbed with his final thrusts making deep contractions pulse rapture from her center to the tips of her fingers. Deaf, dumb, blind, she could only feel. She was in heaven.

CHAPTER ELEVEN

RAOUL HAD NEVER feared for his life during sex, but tonight came pretty close. His heart still felt as though it was under enormous pressure. Taxed. Too full.

Sitting on the foot of the bed, he wanted to believe a trip to the cardiologist would fix him, but it wasn't the answer. The woman avoiding his gaze as she pulled the green gown over her head and let it fall into place was the shard of glass piercing his chest.

"Are you all right?" he asked, voice burning like whiskey in his throat.

"Of course." She flipped her hair free of the gown and bent her attention to the narrow zipper along her side.

She'd been the one to hear the chime announcing a text from her sister while he'd been brain-dead from the most powerful orgasm in history. His legs wouldn't hold him, his skin wanted nothing but the silken brush of Sirena's smooth nudity and all his libido could think was *more.*

This sort of dependence scared the hell out of him, making him want to retreat, maybe do some work for a few hours. Definitely remove himself from her presence until he'd recovered his equilibrium.

At the same time, he was disturbed by Sirena's emotional withdrawal. She'd been as caught up as he, it had been incredible, but now she was subtly tense, offering to text the limo driver to pick them up.

He did it, then said what was top of mind before he thought better of it. "I'm not ready to share you. Maybe if we stayed in here a week—"

Like magic, her force field of aloofness fell away and a sweet smile appeared. "If these breasts were detachable, I'd send them ahead and have the driver collect the rest of me tomorrow."

The medieval clamp on his heart eased. Her humor made it easy to amble across to smooth her hair off her shoulder and admit, "That was incredible. Thank you."

"I thought so, too." Her tiny voice tightened the follicles all over his body.

But the way she shyly ducked her head made this all feel too fleeting. He wanted this new circumstance locked into place. Couldn't she see how simply right this was?

"We're getting married," he said with quiet assertion.

Sirena felt something in her ease. She'd been quietly fighting terror that paradise would swing one-eighty into hell again, but his arrogant order let her know he wasn't planning to dump her as quickly as he'd seduced her. Still, she didn't hear anything about love and that tightened her heartstrings to a point near breaking.

Reminding herself they'd come a long way and she shouldn't expect too much, she said lightly, "Let me guess. I have two choices? Say yes now or say yes later?"

He blinked, not revealing what was going on in his quicksilver brain.

"Do you want to say no?" His instant air of detachment pushed her heart to the edge of a plank, but she supposed he could be having as much difficulty dropping his defense mechanisms as she was.

"No." The word came out a bit forlorn. Never had she imagined marrying a man who didn't love her, but if he couldn't see himself having sex with anyone else, she couldn't see herself marrying anyone else. There were enough bonuses to balance the limitations, she promised herself.

"Then it's settled," he said.

She bit lips that wouldn't stop trembling.

They reached the penthouse and Ali eagerly perched across from her in the lounge, practically bouncing with excitement as Sirena sat down to feed Lucy.

"Well?" Ali demanded.

"Well, what?" Sirena asked, inwardly tracking Raoul to the bar.

"Oh, you're hopeless. Raoul, did you propose or didn't you?"

He paused with his glass half raised to his lips, gaze flicking to Sirena's.

"We decided to marry, yes," Sirena said with as little inflection as she could manage.

"I *told* you a man doesn't go all out like this without a ring in his pocket. Let's see it." Ali clapped her hands then held them out, wiggling her fingers to coax Sirena to show her own.

"I—"

To her right, she heard the bottom of a glass hit the bar top with a firm *clunk,* but she refused to look in his direction.

"Sweetie, we have a baby," she said to Ali. "Getting married is a formality. I don't need an engagement ring for the few days it will take to get a license and sign some papers."

"You're not having a real wedding? But you always planned the full dress and fancy cake and Dad walking you down the aisle—"

"I was a kid when I talked like that! No, listen." She hurried to forestall her sister beating this particular dead horse. "Dad and Faye have made it plain they're not up to traveling and Raoul has lost a lot of time with Lucy coming early. It was very sweet of him to arrange for us to have this visit—" she made a point to let him see she was utterly sincere in her appreciation of that, but his inscrutable expression and unmoving stature cowed her "—but we don't need any more disruptions," she finished.

Ali didn't want to let it go, that was her nature. She might be nineteen, but she was still a little girl in some respects. Sirena had grown up enough to realize you had to move past childish dreams and be realistic. She got Ali to drop it and Raoul left the room.

It was Ali's last night, so Sirena wasn't entirely sorry they'd been called back early. She settled Lucy, took off her makeup, then she and Ali had tea and talked about the stars Sirena had rubbed elbows with. Deep inside, she hugged close the secret of all that had happened with Raoul. Ali would never understand if she told her how far they'd come, but the closeness they'd achieved was huge. No brilliantly cut chunk of stone or fancy frock would ever mean as much to her as the way he'd held her as if he didn't want to let her go.

It was late when they finally said good-night and sought their beds.

Sirena came up short as she found hers occupied.

Raoul set aside his tablet as she stopped inside her door. The lamps slanted golden light across his bare chest, making a relief map of his muscled shoulders and abdomen. She couldn't decipher everything in his austere expression, but there was no mistaking the possessiveness of his quick glance from her lapels to her naked legs.

Tremendous self-consciousness struck. Playing with the tie of her kimono, she tried for nonchalance as she said, "I didn't know you were waiting for me."

"I was trying to fix that situation in Milan." His scowl

told her he was still trying. "I'll give my schedule a hard look and figure out when we can get to Australia. Do you want to put off the wedding until then?"

"No," she said firmly, hurrying to the bathroom to brush her teeth, hoping he'd take it as a signal to end the subject, but he didn't. When she returned to the bedroom, he continued as if she hadn't left.

"I've booked a jeweler to bring some engagement rings before we have to drop Ali at the airport."

"I won't wear one." The words came out with more vehemence than she meant, but the sort of wedding she'd always dreamed of had been a celebration of love and this relationship wasn't that soul mate connection. Yes, she loved him and he'd come a long way toward showing more than lust for her, but going through all the hoops and barrels of a big wedding would feel fake. It was vitally important they keep things as honest as possible considering their rough start.

He had one knee crooked beneath the sheet and one strong wrist braced on its point. "Do you intend to wear a wedding band?" His tone held a stealthy note of danger that made her tummy flutter.

She was shocked by how defenseless yet wonderful the idea of wearing his wedding band made her feel. An engagement ring was a romantic gesture; a wedding band was a lifetime commitment. Her throat thickened and she grew warm all over as she murmured, "Of course."

Trying to cloak how disturbed she was, she clicked off the lamp and gestured toward the one on his side.

He didn't move. "Why won't you wear an engagement ring, then?"

"Jewelry with stones isn't practical around babies. And—" She hugged herself. A tiny part of her still hated for him to think she was avaricious, but it was more than that. "I'm not interested in being a bride. I just want us to be a family."

His unapproachable vibes dissipated. He reached to flick the sheet back, motioning her into the bed beside him. She hesitated, unable to be casual despite how intimate they'd been a few hours ago. He was naked and despite her exhaustion, she was dying to feel him against her, but shedding her robe as if they'd always been sleeping like this was impossible.

Amusement curled his masculine lips into a sardonic smile. "Really?" He turned away to click off the light.

"Don't laugh," she grumbled as the darkness made it safe to drop her robe and slide into bed.

Warm hands pulled her into contact with his hot, ready body. "I have better things to do than laugh, Sin."

They married in Las Vegas on the way back to New York. Sirena made all the arrangements over the internet and this time, when they were given a shared room at his mother's, she didn't hesitate. Despite the perfunctory ceremony, the state of being married felt surprisingly natural.

They fell easily into old patterns. Within days of returning to London, Raoul had talked her into giving up her transcription customers and taking charge of his personal calendar instead. It came with an allowance similar to her old salary, which was rather generous considering her flat was paying for itself in rent and she didn't have any other living expenses. Still, taking his money needled her. It would probably be healthier for them if she remained financially independent, but she accepted because she loved being part of his day-to-day life.

"And hire me a decent PA, would you?" he added as they finished up breakfast one of their first mornings back.

"Perhaps they have a two-for-one special at the nanny agency," she mused, flicking the screen on her tablet, not looking up even though she was aware of him pausing after rising from the table.

"Do you think you're funny?" he asked above her in the ominous tone that used to make her quake, but now made her grin.

"You just handed me a list that includes booking you a play date—" for squash, but she overlooked that "—and buying your mother a birthday gift. Throw in a nappy change and I'm spot-on."

He was silent, then said, "This is the sort of thing you used to say in your head when you were afraid I would fire you if you said it aloud?"

She kept her chin tucked and lifted only her lashes. "I'm just having fun, Raoul."

"Are you?" She knew him well enough to recognize when he was completely serious, but she was distracted by the way his stern natural handsomeness gave him an air of commanding masculine authority. Her nerve endings came alive in tingling pulses and the rest of her wanted to melt into a puddle of undying adoration.

"Yes," she croaked, and tried to clear the huskiness from her throat, not quite remembering what they were talking about.

"Because there was a time when I planned to offer you a position on my executive. If you'd rather pursue your career, you can have a job with me and it won't be nepotism. You're qualified. Or look for something else that appeals. I would hate trying to navigate the two schedules," he said with a significant pause to let the downside sink in, "but we could make it work if this isn't challenging enough for you."

She warmed, wistful about the reasons her promotion had never come about, but she wasn't sure she would have taken it even if he had offered it. With her nose wrinkled in self-deprecation, she admitted, "I like working directly with you, being part of the action without having to take the lead. It makes me feel needed. Is that bad?"

"You are needed." He nodded at their daughter in her bouncy chair. "By both of us. If I took you for granted before she came along, well, rest assured I came to realize what I'd lost and very much appreciate all you do for me now."

She softened all over. Her smile wouldn't stay pinned. "Thank you for that."

He bent to steal a swift kiss that turned into a lingering one, sweet as molasses. As he straightened and gathered his things, he added, "And you should know by now that my fantasies run to sexy secretaries over naughty nannies."

She was so in love it was hard to remember he didn't feel the same.

Working for him, she had been one of many distant moons in his dynamic orbit. Now she was a part of his world in a way she hadn't expected could happen. Raoul didn't try to cram her into a corner of his busy life. He made a space for her and Lucy that gave them priority over everything else. When work demanded his time outside the office, he made every effort to include her, keeping her firmly at his side, not the least awkward about the fact she used to be his PA.

Tonight's cocktail party was different from an award ceremony or the meet and greet he'd had with his new clients last week, though. No one there had known she used to be his employee. Here, the hosts would likely remember her as the girl with the quick-draw tablet and Bluetooth earplug who had brought them coffee and arranged their lunch.

Sirena braced herself when Paolo Donatelli, an international banker, and his wife, Lauren, welcomed them into the luxurious foyer of their Milan penthouse. They were a stunning couple, Paolo casually elegant in a gorgeously Italian way, his wife tall and warmly glowing in the family way.

"Congratulations on your happy news! You took everyone by surprise. Even Paolo," Lauren said, kissing both Sirena's cheeks.

"You're misquoting me, *bella*," Paolo said, copying his wife's affectionate gesture toward Sirena. "I said if you two were involved, no one would know unless Raoul wanted it known. He's the most discreet man I've ever met."

Sirena blushed, throat going dry as she felt their curiosity for more details on how their marriage and baby had slid under the radar the way they had.

"We surprised ourselves," Raoul said, drawing her closer as he looked into her eyes. The reassurance in his gaze warmed her, easing her past the discomfiting moment. "And discretion is what you pay for, Paolo," he added, neatly halting further prying.

"This is true," the Italian said wryly. "On that note..."

The men disappeared into Paolo's study. Before Lauren drew Sirena into the gaggle of guests, she clasped her arm. "Did we put you on the spot? I'm sorry. The truth is, I'm thrilled. I don't always feel a connection to the spouses of Paolo's associates, but you've always been so nice. I'm glad I'll be seeing more of you."

"Don't think I won't cash in on that," Sirena said, relaxing as she sensed a genuine offer of friendship. "I'm dying to shop with you. You always look amazing and here I am in Milan, but I don't speak Italian."

Lauren's eyes widened in excitement. "I would love that!"

It was the boost of acceptance she needed. Lauren also helped her find her own style, so Sirena's confidence grew as she spent more time on Raoul's arm. Their days were busy and their nights incredible, building tiny bridges of connection she began to trust were sturdy and reliable.

That developing sense of closeness and familiarity brought her into his London office tower one afternoon simply because she was missing him.

"Hello," she said, using her weight to press the door shut behind her while she took in the familiar sight of him at his massive desk against the wall of windows, London's skyline behind him.

"This is an unexpected pleasure." He leaned back.

"Lucy had her photo shoot this morning. I wanted to show you the proofs. It could have waited, but since I was only a few blocks away…" She dug the flash drive from her coat pocket as she came around to the side of the desk where the outlets were mounted. "And I wanted to see your face when you see them rather than—oh!"

Tumbled into his lap, she took a breathless second to figure out how she'd wound up here. As if there was any mystery, when her husband was looking at her as though he wanted to eat her alive. An appreciative smirk twitched his mouth while an intriguing tension made his cheekbones taut.

"Where's Lucy?" He drew the chopsticks from her hair so her waves tumbled free.

Grinning, she toyed with the knot of his tie. "Watching her new nanny try to flirt with your new PA, completely oblivious to the fact she's barking up the wrongly oriented tree."

"Lucy or the nanny?" He released the zip on her calf-length boot and slipped his hand inside. His warm touch cupped her calf then circled to fondle her knee.

She purred, losing track of the conversation. Settling into him a little more, she felt the press of his growing arousal. His light caress climbed to the side of her thigh beneath her suede skirt. When she pressed her lips into his throat, she felt him swallow.

"Did you lock the door?" His hand was well under her skirt now, moving insistently beneath the tight, unforgiving cut, delving to the top of her leg.

"A detail-oriented girl like me? What do you think?"

"I think I'm about to lose all ambition for the rest of the day." He bent his head to kiss her and the phone rang. The heat flaring in his eyes sparked to frustration. "Only you and my mother have that line."

"I might be pocket-dialing you, if that's my phone digging into my hip."

He chuckled, "Smart-ass," and leaned to tap the button for speakerphone. "Mother?" he prompted.

"Yes, it's me."

"Good timing. Sirena is here." The ironic face he made had her catching back laughter with a hand against her mouth.

They exchanged pleasantries before his mother got to the reason for her call: a misplaced bracelet.

"I know it's silly to ask if you remember seeing where I left it, but I've been up and down through the house and it hasn't turned up."

Raoul flashed a glance to Sirena. It was a quick, unexpected slide of a knife between her ribs, barbed with *Again?*

He recovered quickly, even showed a hint of culpability in the way his gaze wavered and flicked away. "I remember you wearing it to dinner," he said to his mother.

"Sirena?" she prompted.

Her ears rang with all that had just gone unsaid. Her skin chilled and the heart that had been flowering open shriveled to a poisoned husk. The bleak world she had inhabited for so many months crept toward her like dark clouds closing in from the horizon.

"Same," she said through a tight throat, all too aware she'd admired the tennis bracelet openly, listening intently to Beatrisa's story of how touched she'd been to receive it from her son for her sixtieth birthday.

It was all going to start happening again and this time it would hurt even more.

Raoul was aware of his wife turning to marble as he finished with his mother—which he hurried because Sirena's growing tension needed to be addressed. She tried several times to climb off his lap, but he held her in place until he'd ended the call.

"Let me up," she said icily.

"I don't suspect you of taking that bracelet," he growled. Doubt might have flickered through his mind, but he was entitled, wasn't he?

She dug her elbow into the middle of his chest. Her legs determinedly tried to find the floor. "Get your hands off me," she snarled.

He lifted his grip, angry that she was angry. He didn't help her rise, just protected his genitals as she scrambled to her feet and zipped her boot. Flushed, with her hair loose and disheveled, she located her purse and would have walked out without another word.

Leaping up, he met her at the door. "You're not walking out like this."

"Oh, you expect me to stay here and put out so you can accuse me of using my body for leniency again?"

The muscles in his abdomen were so tight there shouldn't have been room for his stomach to compress under a blow, but his gut knotted as though she'd kicked him.

He clenched his fist where he'd braced his arm across the closed door, aware that his wife was incredibly passionate, but the lack of inhibition she showed him was the result of weeks of building on their connection out of bed as much as in it. She still had morning-after blushes and charming as they were, they reminded him that physical intimacy was still new to her. She wasn't capable of using sex for any kind of manipulation. It was purely joy and pleasure for both of them.

"No," he bit out, shamed anew that he'd ever reduced her generous giving of herself to such a low transaction. He knew how much damage his accusation had done to her acceptance of his desire and need for her. Bringing it up again only pushed them farther apart than they already were and he felt a cold, anxious sweat break over him, not wanting to be here in this uncertain place. "I do expect you to talk this out like an adult, though. Not storm off in a fit," he insisted.

"I'm the one reacting badly? Your first thought was that I'd stolen again! I knew you didn't trust me when you set up my account without giving me access to any of yours, but to look at me like that, so blatantly accusing me—"

"You did it once before, damn it. Is it so surprising—"

"Once," she cried, holding up a single finger. "One time I thought I'd lean on someone else's resources instead of trying to do everything myself. It was wrong, I know that, but it was *one time*. Have I taken anything from you before or since? Not even a few bob for nappies from the change on your night table. But you can't wait to find fault! Does it feel good? Does it justify the way you hold back your heart and don't trust me? God, I knew it would be a mistake to get this involved with you!"

She turned away, so she didn't see the way he was knocked back, as if her outburst had been a spray of bullets. He couldn't even defend himself, aware that subconsciously he *was* waiting for a sign that his growing feelings for her were misplaced. She was coming to mean far too much to him. Every time he thought the level of emotion between them was as much as he could handle, his attachment grew. The more you cared, the more you risked and he was getting in so deep there was no self-protection left. He didn't like it, he couldn't deny that.

But to hear her call their relationship a mistake was a brutal blow. He hated seeing her shoulders buckle, hated knowing that she was only standing here in this room with him because he was barring the door.

"Look, the thing with the account I set up for you—"

"I don't want to hear it, I really don't. Would you let me take Lucy home? She needs her nap."

"I'll come home with you." He moved to fetch his laptop. As he did, she walked out. Beyond the door, Lucy let out a sudden cry.

"I'm sorry," the nanny said anxiously as he emerged to find Sirena trying to comfort the baby. "She scratched herself."

An urgent call came in at that second and Sirena wound up leaving without him. When he managed to fight traffic and get home, he was relieved to find them there, even though Sirena was pale and frazzled. Mother and baby were both out of sorts. He was beginning to think Lucy had Sirena's sensitive nature for undercurrents, because she was obviously unsettled by her mother's tension.

He took over soothing the fussy infant and, despite his urgent need to sort things out between them, suggested Sirena take a bath. It was late when they sat down to a quiet dinner, just the two of them. Sirena picked at her food.

The silence built.

"Sin—"

"I don't want to talk about it."

"I called her back," he said, overriding her hostility. "Her housekeeper is sure she saw it on her dresser top after we left. It's fallen behind some furniture or something."

"So it's not that you believe me. You believe the house-keeper."

He drew patience into his lungs with a long inhale. "You barely wear the jewelry I give you and don't spend half the money in the account I opened for you. I have no reason to believe you'd want or need that bracelet."

Her mouth stayed pinched while she rearranged her food.

"I've put what happened behind us. Today was a slipup on my part, that's all."

"Fine," she said in the way women did when they meant, *Like hell,* but he took her at her word, determined to get them back on the comfortable footing they'd been enjoying. When they went to bed, he reached for her as he did every night.

She didn't melt her body into his the way he'd come to expect.

He wanted her. Badly. This break in their connection needed to be reestablished with the physical joining that brought him a kind of pleasure and sense of accord he couldn't even articulate. But while she didn't outright push him away, she didn't open to his kiss and heat to his touch the way she usually did.

With urgency riding him, he slowed his touch, trying to reassure her and himself that nothing had changed. He knew all her trigger points and lightly stimulated them: the dimples at the small of her back that made her shiver, the tendon in her neck that turned her to pudding when he scraped his teeth against it, the underside of her arm that was ticklish, but also made her turn into him and twine her leg around his waist.

When she moaned softly and combed her fingers into his hair, he shuddered with relief, but kept the pace gradual and thorough, wanting her to know how much he revered this bond between them. He didn't know how else to express his feelings for her. They were too deep and disturbing to even try to voice. Surely when they were like this, she felt it and understood?

Her hand moved restlessly on his shoulder and he kissed his way down the inside of her arm. Her wrist was sweetly feminine, the fine pulse beating frantically against his tongue, her fingers trembling against his mouth. He lightly sucked one, then another, anointing all her sensitive places, biting into the mound below her thumb until he'd imprinted himself on her lifeline.

She arched, the seeking signal enough to blast through his control, but he was determined to have every inch of her before she had one inch of him. He rolled her onto her stomach and used his leg to pin hers, then stroked her body with his. Her skin was soft and smooth, her form lovely with its curves and nectarine-scented skin. He kissed his way down her spine as he stroked her legs and buttocks, intensely turned on as she gasped and lifted into his touch and moaned his name.

Pushing the mane of her hair away from her neck, he settled on her, letting her feel how aroused he was. The slam of his heartbeat was like a piston trying to stamp into her. He slid a hand beneath her, cupping her breast then moving lower to the wet heat that was all his.

"I can't get enough of you," he admitted in a hot whisper against her bared ear. "I think about this all the time, giving you pleasure, feeling you melt for me." She was close to shattering, straining beneath him, making gorgeous noises that had the hairs all over his body standing up as he fought losing it without even entering her.

Easing away, he rolled her to face him.

She was trembling, her arms shaking as she tried to draw him over her. Her thighs fell open, but he only kissed down her breastbone to her navel.

"Raoul, I'm dying," she moaned, trying to draw him back up to her.

He was hanging by a thread, but took his time settling on her. Easing into her was like immersing himself in heaven. He went slowly, savoring every heartbeat while fighting the threatening eruption. Catching her inciting hands in his own, he held them still and let her feel him in complete possession of her.

"I will never be careless with you," he told her, deeply aware of the effect he was having on her, the twitch of her thighs scissoring his waist, the clasp of her sheath, the shaken breaths sawing between her lips. "This is too important to me."

He swallowed her gasp as he covered her trembling lips with his, wanting to crush her with all the passionate hunger in him, but venerating her instead, doing everything in his power to transmit that she was pure sweetness, utter joy to him. Perfect.

But he wasn't superhuman. The connection so vital to him was also his lifeblood and he needed to stoke it. The withdrawal and thrust sent a wave of intense pleasure down his back, pulling him tighter and harder, making the need to drive himself into her unbearable. He basked in the sheer magnificence of her, moving with gentle deliberation as he savored the effect she had on him, the way she responded to his strokes.

Their struggle was long and slow and deep. Impossible to give up and impossible to prolong. When the high keening noise came into her throat and her teeth closed on his earlobe, when her climax was only a breath away, he let himself fall, his wife clutched firmly in his arms.

CHAPTER TWELVE

As Raoul knotted his tie, he wasn't sure if he should feel smug or sorry. Over his reflected shoulder, Sirena was motionless on their ravaged bed, deeply asleep.

Last night had been intense. Even after he'd fetched Lucy for a feed a couple of hours ago and come back fully expecting they'd both finally catch a few winks, Sirena had reached for him as though they hadn't been colliding all night. They'd nearly killed each other with the force of their most recent release.

Then they had finally passed out. When his body had woken him out of habit at six, he'd considered canceling today's meetings, but two very in-demand people had flown in on his request. He had to make time for them.

He didn't like leaving Sirena without saying goodbye, but he was loath to wake her when he was the reason she needed her rest. Shrugging on his suit jacket, he moved closer to gauge how deep into REM she was.

Her face was contorted with agony and her limbs gave a twitch of sleep-paralyzed struggle. Alarmed, he sat to grasp her shoulder, sharply saying, "Sin!" to snap her awake.

"Nooo!" she cried and her hand came up so fast it caught him in the mouth before he knew it.

"What the hell?" He dabbed a finger against his lip, expecting she'd split it.

Her wild eyes came to rest on him, terror slowly receding as she curled her offending hand into her chest. "Did I hit you? Oh, my God, I'm so sorry." Her horror was as real as the remnants of panic still whitening her lips.

"You were having a nightmare. What was it?"

Shadows of memory crept into her eyes before she shielded them with her lashes. Without enlightening him, she drew the blankets up to her neck, shivering and looking to the clock. "What time is it? I didn't realize it was so late. Did your alarm go off?"

"Sin?" He smoothed her hair away from her sweaty temple. "Tell me."

"I don't want to think of it. Will you check Lucy while I have a quick shower?"

"You should sleep in."

"I don't want to try in case it comes back." She slid from the far side of the bed, leaving him uneasy.

Despite the passion that remained acute as ever between them, Sirena couldn't shake the sense of an ax about to fall. She brushed aside her worries by day, telling herself to trust that Raoul really had put his suspicions away, but her subconscious tortured her at night. He woke her from horrible nightmares at least once a night, bleak, frightening dreams where he wrenched Lucy from her arms and condemned Sirena to utter abandonment. Sometimes she was in prison, sometimes she was outside his gates, rain soaking her to the skin, cold metal numbing her fingers, his feelings for her completely beyond her reach.

He'd reassure her and be considerate and affectionate and would make love to her so sweetly she thought she would die, but she still wound up alone and rejected when she closed her eyes.

"I don't know what else I can say," he bit out over a

week later after a sullen dinner when he had remarked on the dark circles under her eyes.

They were in Paris, the city of lovers, sharing after-dinner coffee in the lounge. The nanny had taken an evening off with friends. The housekeeper had tidied up the dishes before leaving for the night. Outside the rain-specked window, the ink-black path of the Seine wound in gilded streaks past the purple and red and yellow lights of the buildings on the far shore.

"Tell me the bracelet has turned up," she said with a melancholy shrug, trying to be dismissive but actually feeling quite desperate.

Thick silence. He'd made her tell him what the dreams were about, but it hadn't helped either of them cope. His lack of response almost sounded accusatory to her.

"It's not like I want to be like this," she pointed out defensively.

Her phone rang in the depths of her purse. She stood to find it, hoping to avoid another dead-end conversation about something she couldn't control.

"You could try trusting me. That's what this comes down to."

She caught back a snort and insisted, "I do," but her heart twisted as though it knew she was lying. What could she do about that? If he loved her, she might be able to believe that he wasn't on the verge of rejecting her. But what he felt for her was passion—and that wasn't a forever type of feeling, was it?

"You don't even trust me enough to talk about this without seizing any excuse to walk away," he said pointedly.

"What is there to say?" She dropped her purse onto the sofa and folded her arms. "I'm supposed to ignore the fact there's no one else it could be? Is your mother losing her memory? Not a bit that I've noticed. Could it be the housekeeper? The one who's been with her for ten years?

Oh, I know, it's Miranda, who gets paid a fortune on top of that trust you set up for her."

A flash of something moved in his eyes. She didn't try to interpret it, too busy rushing on with the facts piled up against her.

"Did a thief break in and steal one bracelet in a house-ful of electronics and art? No! Unless *you* took it, the only other person it could be is *me*." She pointed to her chest. "I'm ready to confess just to get the breakup and court proceedings over with."

A cloak of such tangible chill fell over him, he virtually turned gray and breathed fog. "A divorce? Is that the kind of court proceedings you're referring to?"

Her fingernails clawed into her upper arms. It wasn't, but if he reached for the D-word that quickly, it must be something he was considering. The pain that crept into her then didn't even have a name, it was too all encompassing and deadly.

Into their staring contest, his phone rang. He didn't move, but it broke the spell. She looked away, body pulsing with anguish.

"Is it?" he demanded through his teeth, ignoring his phone.

"How else will you react when it never turns up?" she said in a strained voice.

When she dared to look at him, he was so far inside himself there was no reaching him. It was as if the man who had been her protector and sounding board and part-ner had checked out and left the brute from the end of his driveway.

Her heart retracted into a core of ice, cracking from its own cold density.

His phone went silent and her tablet burbled.

"Oh, for God's sake!" she cried, rounding to the coffee table and glancing at the screen to see it was her sister. A different chill moved into her chest. The timing was wrong for a friendly visit—

She swiped at the screen. "Ali?" she asked before the vision of her sister came into focus, crying.

"It's Dad. He's had a heart attack. Mum's in the ambulance. I'm going to meet them at the hospital."

Sirena wasn't aware of swaying, only felt herself steady as firm hands grasped her and eased her onto the sofa. Raoul caught the tablet as it tumbled from her numb fingers.

"She'll be there as soon as I can make arrangements," he said in a rasping voice, ending the call. He tried to take her hands, but Sirena jerked from his touch, practically leaping to her feet.

"I have to pack."

"You're in shock."

"I need to do something."

"Fine. I'll order the flight." He ran a hand over his face, looking surprisingly awful. Maybe it was memories of losing his own father.

That thought made her stomach bottom out. Not dwelling on it, she went through the motions of packing, counting nappies for Lucy, fretting about the time it would take to circle half the globe. Would she reach her father in time?

Calling back the nanny didn't make sense. As nice as she was, she wasn't family. Sirena just wanted Raoul. For all their horrid conflict, he was a pillar. She couldn't dismiss how supportive he was as he booked a private jet, bundled them into a limo and buckled Lucy securely beside her in the plane's cabin.

"Text when you land so I know you arrived safely," he said.

"You're not coming?" Her barely there control shredded to near nothing.

"There's something I have to do."

Divorce. The ugly word came back, more noxious than ever. This was it, the expulsion from his life she had feared. Or rather, expected. Bile rose to the back of her throat, sitting in a hot burn despite her convulsive swallow. At least she had Lucy.

Without saying a word, she set her hand on their daughter and looked straight ahead. Funny how after all this time of aching for forgiveness, she didn't care what he believed. She only wanted him to be with her, but he walked away.

As she watched him depart, everything in her was mute and bereft. Minutes later the plane was climbing and the delicate silken ropes binding her to him stretched, thinned and finally snapped.

Forty-eight hours later, the only good news in her life was that her father's surgery had gone well and he would recover in time.

On the other hand, she had a baby who cried if she so much as thought about putting her down. As if the awkwardness of reacquainting with Faye wasn't hard enough without the buffer of her father to smooth the way, her sister insisted on returning to school on the other side of Sydney to be with—*don't tell Mum*—her boyfriend.

"This way you can use my bed," Ali insisted in front of her mother, putting Sirena on the spot. It was Ali's way of being helpful. She was oblivious to the undercurrents.

A cot for Lucy had already been borrowed from the neighbor and Sirena didn't want to appear churlish, but it only took one remark from her stepmother to put Sirena squarely back into her broadly criticized childhood.

"I imagine she'd be sitting up if she wasn't so fat."

Lucy was going to have a figure like her mother's. Not everyone thought that was a problem, Sirena bit back retorting. *Ask my husband.*

Her chest burned as she wondered how long she'd be able to refer to him that way.

He stunned her by contacting her at that moment, through her smartphone.

Highly conscious of her stepmother listening in, she bounced the baby on her hip and tried not to reveal how put out she was that the Wi-Fi she'd scrimped to pay for all those unemployed months, so she could contact her father and sister as often as she liked, had been canceled. *Ali's gone to school. What do we need it for?*

The phone screen was a poor substitute for her tablet and this conversation would cost her a fortune. She felt her scowl and Raoul gave her a forbidding look right back, killing any remote hopes she entertained that they weren't on the skids.

He was in his New York office, the dull sky behind him. His queries about her father and hope for his quick recovery were delivered in a strained rumble that was barely audible over her stepmother bashing dishes.

Sirena could only swallow, such deep emotions were accosting her, and she didn't know what to say with prying, critical ears a few steps away.

"You'll be there until he's released?" Raoul presumed.

"Yes, I—" She was aware of the temperature dropping to arctic levels as Faye absorbed the notion of unwanted houseguests for the indefinite future. "I have a lot to figure out. I'll call you once I know what I'm doing."

"Very well." He sounded about as friendly as Faye.

Ending the call, she endured an oppressive evening where it took everything in her not to reveal her misery and sense of failure to a woman who would dance a jig over her suffering. She barely slept, but when she woke, it was with a fresh sense of purpose.

She was not the unwanted stepchild any longer. Maybe her marriage was a disaster, but she was still a woman with resources and skills. After popping by the hospital to photograph her weak but proud father holding his grand-daughter, she called a real estate agent.

It would be a fresh start in a place that wouldn't remind her of Raoul. An hour later, she was shown into a building under redevelopment.

"This is available immediately?" she asked, thinking that trading on her husband's name had its perks.

"As soon as your credit is approved, hopefully later today," the agent told her.

Money would be tight. She doubted Raoul would con-tinue her allowance if they separated, but she hadn't let on to the agent that a breakup was in the cards. She was using her London flat, which was solely in her name, as leverage. She'd have to rely on transcription to make her payments until she found a decent job, but Raoul had said she had executive potential. She wouldn't sell herself short. None of this would be easy, but living with Faye and her father was not an option and neither was returning to her husband.

She needed her own space. Her heart was breaking into little pieces to match her marriage. She'd always known it wouldn't last, but she still needed solitude to come to terms with it.

After her and Lucy's first night in the quiet of their new flat, they woke early for their morning visit to the hospi-tal. They picked up groceries on the way back and, as a distraction from her misery, invited Faye to see the place. Sirena had concocted a story about Raoul wanting them to have a condo for their visits here, unwilling to confess to her imminent divorce. Unfortunately, that gave Faye carte blanche to show up with paint chips and a pile of unsolicited decorating advice.

"It's just been painted," Sirena argued.

"This oxblood is far too loud for a baby. Look at this eggshell. It will keep her calm. Book the painters to come in after you go back to London. It'll be finished and the fumes gone before your next visit."

She wasn't going back to London.

A knock at the door relieved Sirena from having to explain. She expected the building manager. He had promised to take care of some finishing items today.

As she reached the door, she hoped she could use this excuse to encourage Faye on her way—

"Oh!" Her heart leaped into her throat as she found Raoul outside her door.

He narrowed bleary eyes on her. Bleak lines were carved into his face, barely disguised by a cantankerous expression. When he raked his avaricious gaze down her simple blue capris and collared top, her pulse reacted with a dancing skip, but he looked so forbidding she could only stare dumbly at him.

"I didn't expect you," she said stiltedly.

"No?" He shouldered his way into the tiny flat, taking in the bare walls, the clean but dated furniture and the woman trying to tease a pacifier into his daughter's jabbering mouth.

Faye left off as Raoul approached, coming to attention in the instinctual way most did when confronted with his authoritative presence.

He nodded at her before he set a wide hand on his daughter's tummy. "How are you, kitten?"

Lucy kicked in excitement, grinning toothlessly with recognition and joy, arms flailing.

"I missed you, too," he said, hand staying on her while he took a better look around the flat. Disapproval blazed off him, like sharp, aggressive, glinting knives. No tender welcome or affectionate nickname for her, Sirena noted with a hollow ache.

"You must be the father?" Faye said haughtily when his gaze came back to her.

"My husband, yes," Sirena hurried to interject, pulling herself out of her shock. "Raoul, my stepmother, Faye."

"Nice to meet you," he said without inflection. "Would you be kind enough to watch Lucy while Sirena and I have a private conversation?"

Sirena's stomach hardened into a knot. She could practically hear Faye's, *I told you men expect to make these decisions themselves,* but Faye's opinion was the least of her problems. She hadn't really thought Raoul would give her Lucy, had she?

No, she might have hoped in her heart of hearts that their daughter would be a connection that brought him to her, but this didn't feel as though they were bridging differences. A huge chasm separated them, full of mist and frost.

"I can't walk her in this heat," Faye began, but Raoul negated the suggestion with a flick of his hand.

"We'll be upstairs, viewing the penthouse." His tone was so much that of a confident tycoon, even Faye didn't argue.

Sirena took a moment to set her phone to dial his so Faye could reach them, then accompanied him into the elevator, watching nervously as he punched the P.

"I don't understand—"

"Your agent called to clear your finances and within five minutes was trying to sell me the top floor. It seemed the most expedient way to get into this building if you refused to let me up, so I took the codes and said I'd look at it."

The elevator stopped and her knees weakened. She steeled her spine, but her voice was wobbly. "Of course I'd let you up. We're on perfectly friendly terms."

"Are we?" he rasped, holding the door while she exited, then moving to tap a code into the penthouse's security panel. The half-renovated space was empty of workmen, the concrete floor bare but for a few paint spatters, the walls down to timber frame and the plumbing extracted.

"I can't live with Faye," she blurted, arms flailing defensively. "I've tried to explain how she and I—"

"I understand that," he said with an inscrutable stare. "But you could have gone to a hotel."

She looked away. "That would have been expensive."

"And you weren't about to ask me to cover it, were you?"

Her throat tightened as she tried to swallow, unable to look at him because that topic was just too raw.

"And it would be too temporary," he said in a tone that made her feel wobbly inside. "Because you're staying here. Not coming back to me." It wasn't a question and the graveled way he said it made her flinch.

"There's no point, is there? I realize this seems like I've chosen the farthest place I could get from London, but my family is here, Raoul. Surely you understand why I'd prefer it?" She needed something, someone. They'd never take his place in her heart. The hole was too big, but she couldn't live with this ashen emptiness.

"Oh, I understand." His harsh laugh cut through the tense air. "Run as far from London as you want. I'll follow. If you're adamant about living in that flat you just bought, I'll be in this one."

The words struck like a burst of hot, dusty wind, choking and dry, making her eyes blink. *I'll follow,* but he was following Lucy.

She resisted the desire to rub where her breastbone rang in disappointment. It should be an enormous comfort to her that he hadn't arrived with threats to rend their child from her arms, but all she could think was how jealous she was of her daughter's ability to draw this man's eternal, all-encompassing love.

She might be selfish enough to take their daughter from her father, but he wouldn't separate mother and child.

She touched her brow where it was crinkled, aware of him pacing to the space under the floating staircase near the balcony doors. His footsteps were hollow, everything about this place echoing with the same emptiness she felt. His intention to live here was both pleasure and pain, but she'd had a baby with this man. Their lives would be linked forever. She'd never be given a chance for distance and space and getting over him. They would circle each other for eternity, two planets in the same solar system that never touched.

"Every working cell in my brain is telling me I have no right to keep you from leaving me, but the thought of letting you go makes me sick."

Her heart took a stumbling leap in her chest. She caught back any jumps of joy. It was Lucy he was worrying about losing. Lucy, and maybe a passionate bedmate and a scrupulously organized life.

"I…" She trailed off, realizing she'd been so focused on how anguished she felt, she hadn't noticed how broken he looked. If he'd slept since they'd been in Paris, it hadn't been much. He looked as if he'd aged and his shadow of stubble gave her that same old desire to smooth her hand on his rough cheek.

"Miranda had the bracelet," he spit out, as though the words were so bitter he could hardly keep them in his mouth. "I went to New York to confront her. When you threw her name at me in Paris, I realized immediately it was something she would do. She borrowed it for a night out and forgot to return it." He added in a mutter that his stepsister was a "bloody scatterbrain."

Sirena winced, glad to have the question answered, but in the big scheme of things, what did it matter? He had said he didn't think she'd taken it, but he'd had to go all the way to New York to have it confirmed. That hurt. Blinking, she fought back the burn of head-to-toe agony, willing her mouth to stay steady and the constriction in her chest to ease, but she didn't know what to say.

"No more nightmares, all right?" he said gruffly. "It's resolved. You're not in danger of going to prison. I'm never going to try putting you there and I won't let anyone else do it. Do you understand that, Sirena? That threat is gone. Forever."

His implacable tone and the way he tried to impose his will on her was so endearingly familiar she wanted to cry. She shrugged a fake acceptance, because what did he know about it? She woke up crying because the bed was empty beside her. He wanted to live apart. Her life was missing a giant, ornery, wonderful piece and she could barely stand here absorbing his closeness, knowing they'd never again be *close.*

"I've caused you so much pain, haven't I? And why? Because I was afraid to feel any!" He knocked his fist into his chest with self-disgusted violence, making her start. His ragged voice held her very still, frightened, but not of him. Of how angry he was with himself. He was deeply agonized and it both startled and shook her.

"You were right when you said I was looking for every reason to keep you from affecting me. Your nightmares are my punishment. Tell me they're over now, Sin, because they're beyond anything I can stand. Every night I'm confronted by what a thoughtless, cruel bastard I was to you. How I let you down so grossly. When I think of what I tried to do when you were so fragile, killing yourself to keep our child—"

"Don't," she urged, rushing forward a few steps, anguished by how tormented he was. His remorse was too intense to witness.

"It was worse being away from you, not there to wake

you," he said with a dazed affliction. His voice was like someone whose spirit was dead. "I only left because I wanted the mystery solved once and for all, so you'd finally sleep peacefully again. I was arranging the flight, anxious to get here and ease your mind, when your damned agent called and I learned you never intended to let me share your bed again."

"The dreams weren't that bad—"

"Don't downplay what I did to you!" His near shout made her jump again and he ran a hand over his face, visibly trying to bring himself back under control. "Damn it, do you ever think of yourself? That generosity of yours is exactly what gets to me and makes you necessary in my life every second of every day." His hand came out in a plea. "I've always been aware of it, but I never valued it the way I should have. It's why you risked your job to help your sister. I should have seen you'd never do something like that for personal gain. I didn't need protecting from you. It was the other way around." His face twisted with agony. "Don't let your soft heart forgive me. I don't deserve it. Make me live six floors apart from you and suffer like a soul in hell."

For all the jagged pain in his voice, there was a shred of hope in his eyes. He was looking at her as though she were a lifeline just beyond his reach.

She began to tremble, so confused and shaken she could only blurt, "I *can't*. I want to live with you. You're the one who brought up divorce. You're the one who put me on a plane and sent me away! The nightmares are about you not loving me and I love you so much I can't bear it!" She had to bury her face in her hands then because she was revealing too much. This swell of emotions was too much to hold inside.

Hard hands bit into her arms and she was crushed into his chest. His ragged groan vibrated through her as he held her so hard she thought he'd splice them into hybrid branches on a single trunk. A moan of relief from pain escaped her and she let her hands close on his back in pinching handfuls that had to hurt, but she was ravaged by such deep emotions she needed this embrace to keep from splintering into pieces.

"I love you, Sin. I've been sick without you and all I could think about was my father feeling this way and how deep his pain must have been at not having the woman he loved. It's even worse when I had her and ruined everything…"

"No, you didn't," she moaned and cradled his stubbled face to bring his mouth to hers, cutting off his self-recrimination with a tender kiss, wanting to taste that glorious word he'd used.

He opened his mouth on hers with a groan of greed. Their chemistry flared, but it was so much more. They kissed with aching hunger, shuffling to press tighter, thighs weaving, hips rubbing with shiver-inducing friction.

Cupping her head, he drew his own back, hissing a breath at the ceiling. "I'm not taking you on a damned concrete floor where anyone could walk in."

The landing at the top of the stairs caught his gaze and for a second he considered… When he glanced at his wife, she was bringing her sultry gaze back from the same direction. Her body leaned with heart-swelling pliancy against his.

Tempted nearly to breaking point, he hugged her close and reminded himself how incredibly lucky he was to have this second chance. No way was he screwing it up.

Pressing a kiss to her temple, he said, "I don't deserve you. Let me try to do something right, rather than repeat Oxshott."

Her gaze fell and he feared she took it as rejection, even

though he wasn't able to quit stroking her, filling his hands with the reality of her when he'd been sure they were over.

"I liked Oxshott," she murmured, pouted lips nearly touching his breastbone.

"I loved Oxshott," he said softly, stroking her hair back from her face and looking into her eyes, so moved, so bewildered she could love him, he could barely find words.

"I love you," he repeated, even though it was an inadequate description of the depth of regard and adoration he felt toward her.

A misty look came over her face, but a specter moved behind the gaze she lowered. "You don't have to say it if it's not true. I still want to live with you."

"It's not a conscious choice, Sin," he snorted softly. Looking back on how hard he'd fought against feeling this way put a chill in his blood.

"But you're not happy." Her bottom lip moved unsteadily until she caught it in her teeth.

"It hasn't been a comfortable journey, but right now I couldn't be happier."

Her mouth twitched and she nudged against the erection imprinting her abdomen. Her brow cocked as though to ask, *are you sure about that?*

On the verge of becoming distracted, he cupped her jaw, urging her with a caress of her peach-flushed cheek to look into his eyes. This was too important. He saw the hesitancy and vulnerability she was trying to hide behind her flirty smile. His heart lurched.

"I want to make love to you so much I can hardly breathe." A pleasant shiver chased over him at the mere thought of burying himself in her. "Holding you and touching you is the most incredible experience of my life." He caressed her almost convulsively, reassuring himself that he was touching this beautiful woman who meant so much to him. "I was really scared, Sin. I didn't know how I was going to convince you to give me another shot."

Something stark flashed in her eyes before she ducked her head. "I've loved you from practically the minute we met. You're the only man I'll ever want to be with."

Loyal to a fault and so emotionally brave. He would be a lonely coward if he didn't emulate her.

"And you're the only woman I can imagine spending my life with. You believe that, don't you?" he prompted, rather desperate to know her subconscious wouldn't put her through the wringer ever again.

"Of course," she said, adding cheekily, "I have Lucy."

"Don't joke." He leaned back a fraction, waiting for her chastised gaze to come up to his. "I mean it. I want to spend my life with you. I want to marry you. A proper wedding this time. Your dad can give you away…"

She shook her head, trying to forestall him.

"Why not?" he demanded. "You don't want to be the center of attention?" It was the only excuse he could accept. He wouldn't force her into something that made her uncomfortable.

"Those romantic dreams were a young girl's rescue fantasy." She waved them away as she disentangled herself from his embrace. "I've grown up, got my head on straight. I don't need some empty gesture because you feel guilty. I'm fine. We're fine." Her smile was soft and lovely and tried hard to disguise a deep insecurity.

He stared at her, aware he only had himself to blame. "You still don't trust me," he accused gently.

"Of course I do."

"You don't believe my feelings for you are as strong as yours are for me." He was insulted to the core by that, but this wasn't about him. It was about the fragile self-worth he'd damaged too many times.

"I—" What could she say? It was true. "I'm not trying

to start a fight. I know things will only get better from now on."

He allowed the conversation to end there and they returned to Lucy, then went to the hospital for an introduction to her father. By the time they crawled into bed, she truly felt they were on their way to a stronger relationship than ever. He made love to her with the same sweet power as always and held her all night long.

And then he took over in that mildly annoying way of his, throwing Faye for a loop, checking to see if their house needed modifications for when her father came home. He had a man-to-man chat with her father about his finances, too.

"Don't hurt his pride," she urged before he left for the hospital, and got a pithy look.

"I want him to know he has a fallback if he doesn't get on his feet right away. I take care of my family," Raoul said.

For the first time in a very long time, she began to feel she had a cohesive family. With her confidence renewed in her position as a mother and his wife, she tried to let go of her baggage and enjoy her time with her father and sister. Faye became someone she shook her head over, rather than taking her words to heart, especially after her father remarked on their relationship.

"After your mother died, I saw you growing up so fast, trying to take on all her responsibilities. I married the first woman who looked like she'd have me, hoping to give you back your childhood, but it didn't work. You two never connected. You were so independent. Faye didn't know what to make of you. Moving here, I honestly didn't think you'd miss us or that it would be so long until I saw you again. You sounded happy with your job and traveling…"

Startled by this view of herself, she asked Raoul later, "Do I take charge of everything?"

"You've taken over the renovations of the penthouse."

"You told me to—oh!" She caught a glimpse of the grin he was suppressing and gave him a little shove.

He snagged his arm around her and warmed her with an admiring look. "You're smart and confident and good at anything you chose to do. Which might threaten some men, but I need that sort of inner strength in my wife. It's reassuring to me that you won't give up and drop out on me."

"No, never," she promised.

In fact she felt more integral and necessary to him all the time. He changed the access on all his accounts so they were joint holdings and made it her job to keep everything balanced. She reeled under the depth of responsibility and trust he was showing in her.

Perhaps they were going to make it after all.

By the end of the following week her father was well into his recovery and they were winding up their visit. They were keeping the penthouse for future visits, planning two a year at least, but Raoul really did work best out of London. Everything was returning to a steady, reliable keel and if she felt a little wistful each time he said he loved her, she told herself to be grateful he was able to say the words, even if he didn't mean them the way she did.

The day before they were to leave, Sirena woke late. Raoul had pulled his favorite trick of stealing both baby and monitor, but since he'd been rather passionate last night, not seeming able to get enough of her, she appreciated the extra sleep. Her body was a teensy bit achy in the best possible way, making her feel sensual and well loved even as she was disturbed by the memory of his near-frenetic hunger for physical connection.

Was something wrong? She went looking for him, and reassurance, as soon as she rose.

The flat was small, so it was easy to find him in the lounge, where a muted instrumental was playing, giving the sunny room a lazy Sunday feel. He'd bought her flowers yesterday, enough for three vases, filling the room with splashes of color.

He was closing the main door and had a royal-blue garment bag in his hand. As he moved to drape it over the back of the sofa, he saw her. "Good morning."

Did he sound extra serious? Her tummy gave a flutter of apprehension.

"Good morning. Where's Lucy?" she asked, bending her brow at the fancy logo on the bag. What was it?

"Ali just took her upstairs."

"To the penthouse? Why? I thought we were all having lunch—"

The way he approached, all serious looking in his crisp white shirt and perfectly creased pants, gave her another hitch of anxiety. He was so damned good-looking, freshly shaved and with his new haircut—something he'd sought out himself yesterday without asking her to book it. Very out of character.

In fact, lots of odd details were adding up in her mind to something going on that was being kept from her.

He took her hands and she almost pulled them away, suddenly quite worried, but not sure of what. All her inner signals of conspiracies and loss were firing.

Don't, she told herself, forcing herself to trust him by letting her fingers relax in the firm grasp of his.

He frowned at how chilly her hands were. Emotion seemed to catch at him in a way he couldn't control, causing a flinch across his features. The line of his closed lips wasn't entirely steady and for a second he seemed to struggle to meet her eyes. When he did, her heart bottomed out.

This was big. Whatever it was, it was big and scary.

"What's wrong?" she whispered.

"You're so beautiful," he said, as if it hurt him.

She shook her head. Not right now she wasn't, wearing

only a robe that had taken a splash of coffee yesterday, eyes still smudged with last night's makeup, hair tousled from their extensive lovemaking. Her lips were chapped, her—

Stop it, she told herself. If he said she was beautiful, she had to believe that to him she was. It was just so hard when he looked so uncharacteristically hesitant.

"Raoul?" she prompted.

"I'm not trying to be mysterious, Sin. I'm nervous as hell. I—well, there's nothing to say except…" He released her and took a half step back.

She closed her hands into fists, drawing them tight into her stomach, where serpents seemed to be writhing.

To her eternal shock, he drew something from his pocket and lowered to one knee. Holding out a ring pinched between his finger and thumb, he said, "Will you marry me?"

Sunlight glanced off the diamond, throwing rainbow sparkles into her vision. The moment was imprinted for all time: the delicate notes of music behind the question, the perfume of freesias and roses, the way her heart began to pound with sheer joy, the naked feelings in Raoul's beloved face as he looked up at her: desire, regard, admiration.

She realized she couldn't speak because she'd clapped her hands over her mouth. "We're already married," she reminded him from behind them.

"I want to marry you properly. Everyone is upstairs waiting for us."

Her eyes grew wet as she goggled at him.

"I know you didn't want this," he continued. His voice seemed to come from very deep in his chest. "But I need to know you want to be married to me as much as I love being married to you. I've spoken to your father, told him everything, asked him for your hand…"

"You what?" she gasped. Her heart tried to jump from

her chest. She was both touched and alarmed, unable to process it.

"He took his time thinking about it, and I don't blame him." His shoulders took on a weighted slant. "If I could go back and change things…but I can't. I know why you think I married you. I know you think I'm only trying to assuage guilt. I'm not. Although it would certainly reassure me if you said yes in spite of everything I've done."

The regret in his eyes was too painful to face.

"Don't," she murmured, moving forward to graze her hands over his ears, startled when he locked his arm around her and pressed his face into her middle.

"You will make even the most impossible relationships work so you can stay in the lives of the people you love. I know that about you, Sin." Anguish seemed to hold him in a paroxysm that nearly suffocated her, but she only held him tighter. "You'll be tempted to say yes to me today simply because you hate letting me down. But I can't bear you thinking my love for you is impossible, that what I feel for you isn't real."

"I—" Her arms involuntarily loosened and he surged to his feet, grasping her by the shoulders and compelling her with the force of his personality to take heed.

"I *love* you. This isn't pandering to your romantic side—even though I love the idea of making your dreams come true. It's me asking you to marry me properly. Not for Lucy's sake, but because we love each other. If you don't want that, if you don't believe we're equally invested in this relationship, then don't do it."

He was right, she couldn't imagine hurting or humiliating him with refusal.

He seemed to read her mind as he straightened to look down his nose at her. "Don't marry me out of pity or a sense of obligation. I'd rather a hit of revenge. But, Sin, think about it. Why would I set myself up for this kind of drubbing unless I wanted to prove something to you? Something really important."

Like what?

The truth revealed itself like a specter condensing from something she had tried too hard to see.

"You shouldn't have to prove anything to me. I should just believe you. Trust you," she said, smothered by growing compunction. "That's what I always wanted from you, faith in my feelings and intentions toward you..." She pressed her lips together so hard her chin crinkled. Why hadn't she put it together before this? "I'm so sorry."

"We're not holding grudges, Sin." He stroked a tender hand down her cheek. "This is our fresh start."

She nodded agreement, letting him draw her into his embrace. With her head on his chest, she said, "I love you so much. It's hard to believe you could feel this same way for me. It's so big and endless and you are so incredible. You deserve to be loved like that, but I'm just me."

"If you could see yourself the way I do. The way we all do. You're such an amazing woman, Sin. So strong, but so kind. I'm proud that you're my wife. I want the world to know how much you mean to me."

For such a naturally circumspect man, this was quite an act. She couldn't think of any reason he would do such a public thing, take such a risk, except that he loved her.

She was so overwhelmed and touched she could only wrap her arms around him and hold on, trying to keep the bursting sensations from breaking her skin.

"Will you?" he asked, kissing her hair. "Marry me?"

She nodded through happy tears. "Of course. I'd love to. I love you, Raoul."

"And wear my ring this time," he grumbled, easing back to thread it onto her finger. It was a band of baguette diamonds, smooth enough that the claws wouldn't catch on baby clothes or skin, stunning enough to make her gasp as she really took it in.

"I might have been overcompensating," he commented sheepishly.

"You think?" She laughed, then looked up at him. "I don't know how to handle being this happy." Her cheeks ached from her huge smile. "It means so much to me."

It wasn't the proposal; it was knowing he loved her that made her misty with emotion. She felt his lips touch hers as she blinked fast, trying to keep her eyes from overflowing.

"Ali helped me set it up. I hope our day is everything you imagined your wedding day would be."

It was already better than she'd ever dared hope, but she was still awed by the small touches that made her wedding ceremony utterly perfect. As she was too curvy for ruffles or a full skirt, Ali had found her a gown of lace over silk with a modest train. She did her own hair and makeup, only calling in Ali at the last minute to help her with the veil. Faye loaned her the blue cameo pendant that had been in her family for ages and her father met her at the elevator, still unsteady, but so proud to walk with her. Her heart soared.

When she saw her daughter in a confection of a flower-girl dress sitting on Amber's knee, she almost tripped. Then Raoul's mother and stepsister came into focus and some of their longtime work associates…

He had really laid himself on the line with this arrangement.

Now in a morning suit that took her breath, he turned to her with such unashamed adoration in his eyes, she couldn't speak. Unbelievably moved by their vows, feeling the sincerity deep in her heart as they spoke them, she knew he loved her. *Her.*

And they had a lifetime ahead of them.

He lifted her veil and she kept her eyes open, wanting him to see the same devotion in her gaze as she found reflected in his. They sealed their promises to each other with a tender kiss.

* * * * *

Mills & Boon® Hardback

February 2014

ROMANCE

MEDICAL

Mills & Boon® Large Print

February 2014

ROMANCE

HISTORICAL

MEDICAL

0114 GEN STD LP

Mills & Boon® Hardback
March 2014

ROMANCE

A Prize Beyond Jewels	Carole Mortimer
A Queen for the Taking?	Kate Hewitt
Pretender to the Throne	Maisey Yates
An Exception to His Rule	Lindsay Armstrong
The Sheikh's Last Seduction	Jennie Lucas
Enthralled by Moretti	Cathy Williams
The Woman Sent to Tame Him	Victoria Parker
What a Sicilian Husband Wants	Michelle Smart
Waking Up Pregnant	Mira Lyn Kelly
Holiday with a Stranger	Christy McKellen
The Returning Hero	Soraya Lane
Road Trip With the Eligible Bachelor	Michelle Douglas
Safe in the Tycoon's Arms	Jennifer Faye
Awakened By His Touch	Nikki Logan
The Plus-One Agreement	Charlotte Phillips
For His Eyes Only	Liz Fielding
Uncovering Her Secrets	Amalie Berlin
Unlocking the Doctor's Heart	Susanne Hampton

MEDICAL

Waves of Temptation	Marion Lennox
Risk of a Lifetime	Caroline Anderson
To Play with Fire	Tina Beckett
The Dangers of Dating Dr Carvalho	Tina Beckett

BP